SOUL AND SHADOW

SUSAN MCLEOD

ISBN 978-0-6151-7844-8

Disclaimer:
This is a work of fiction which is meant foremost to be entertaining. Although I have studied ancient Egypt for many years, I do not claim to be an expert. I hope the reader will forgive any historical inaccuracies that may have occurred. Language and place-names have been modernized for ease of reading.

"I have journeyed over a long road. The road of souls is opened. Ye shall not hold captive my soul. Ye shall not keep in durance my shadow. The way is open to my soul and to my shadow."
DECREE: If this Chapter be known by the deceased, he shall come forth by day, and his soul shall not be kept captive.
From The Egyptian *Book of the Dead*

Acknowledgements:

I found much valuable information in the beautifully written and illustrated *Ancient Egypt*, by Lorna Oakes and Lucia Gahlin, and *Egypt: Land of the Pharaohs Revealed*, by Global Book Publishing. *Deadly Doses: A Writer's Guide to Poisons* by Serita D. Stevens with Anne Klarner was a fascinating read. There are many wonderful websites on ancient Egypt, some of which are included on my web page at www.freewebs.com/susanjmcleod.

My family (hi Mom!), friends and co-workers were a great help to me. And Mark, I wouldn't have written this without you. Thanks for everything.

Cover by Heidi Michaels

To Dad, who is always with us.

Chapter One

"Sit down, and I'll tell you a story."

Little did I know how much those simple words were going to change my life.

Amisihathor was living on in eternity. Her name was on everyone's lips—at least, those who could pronounce it. The rest just called her Ami, and they had eagerly awaited her arrival from the Cairo Museum. It was a big day when the mummy finally came to town.

I was one of the first in line to see her, ancient history being my field of study.

A special display had been constructed: a replica of a tomb from the fabled banks of the Nile. Floodlights took the place of the burning Egyptian sun, but when they shone on the honey-colored stone, the effect was much the same. Shadows beckoned from within, mysterious and enticing. I could almost believe, as I stepped through the entryway, that I was actually walking back in time…

"Yeck!"

The spell was broken by a group of schoolchildren already inside. As my eyes adjusted to the dimness, I could see a series of pictures explaining the process of mummification. The kids were poring over the gory details with delight.

"They pulled the brains out through the nose!" said a boy, clearly wishing he could have been there to see the process. "Awesome!"

"And they put their livers in jars!" A young girl stared at the canopic containers. "Are they still there?" she asked.

"Maybe." The boy grinned impishly. "Maybe the mummy will be coming back to get it!"

A teacher shushed the squealing and scuffling children, and herded them away. I moved to the glass cases holding items from everyday life along the Nile. A loaf of petrified bread that was meant to be someone's dinner over three thousand years ago. Eating utensils. Little clay pots that still held traces of eye makeup. Lots of beautiful jewelry: necklaces, amulets, and charms. Just as in today's world, in the ancient one, you needed all the protection you could get.

I lingered a while before going into the inner chamber of the exhibit. This was where Amisihathor lay in state. Her wooden sarcophagus was a work of art. Its colors were as vibrant as when they were first painted, showing the spells and divine beings necessary to guide her into the afterlife. Her spirit had long since flown away. Now, only the mummy remained, wrapped in her yellowed linen. A strange feeling came over me as I gazed at her. An image entered my mind of a living, breathing woman, someone who was talking, eating, worrying, and dreaming. There was something melancholy and a little undignified about her remains being here on display.

As if echoing my thoughts, I heard a woman nearby say firmly to her companion, "That's why I'm being cremated!"

Still, Ami was helping to resurrect a whole civilization. And the ancient Egyptians believed that as long as someone's name was spoken, their soul lived on. So, she should be happy.

A sudden voice in my ear startled me. "She never imagined that she would lie in a place like this," it said. "Her dream was to enjoy eternity in the Field of Reeds with her beloved. Now, she walks in the shadows, waiting."

I looked over my shoulder. A tiny woman was gazing at the mummy sadly. She was thin, but her posture was straight and proud. She looked about as old as the pyramids themselves, and also had a suggestion of their strength and power. This didn't stop me from wondering if she was crazy.

I smiled nervously and began to inch away, but the woman moved with me. I've been told that I have a kind face. It must be true, because I attract strange people like a magnet. And I find it next to impossible to be rude, which has led to some very odd conversations.

"I'm glad I've found you, Lily," my new friend said. She had a British accent with a pleasant, musical quality. "Sit down, and I'll tell you a story."

"Excuse me," I replied reasonably, "but I'm afraid we've never met. And I have to be going now."

She looked at me inquiringly. "You are Lily Evans, research assistant to Professor Peter Briggs, aren't you?"

"Yes," I said, startled that she knew me, "but—"

"Then you're the one. Come along." She waved a hand imperiously.

I can't explain why I followed her. I should have gone the other way and alerted security that a confused old woman was on the loose. But I didn't. Perhaps it was my sympathetic nature, or the commanding look she had in her eye, or simple curiosity. Whatever the reason, I found myself trailing after her, back to the outside of the exhibit and the benches in front of the tomb.

She settled herself on the hard stone like a queen taking her throne. She was amazingly spry for her age, attired in a plain white linen suit and some lovely New Kingdom-style jewelry. I admired a golden bracelet with a scarab clasp. Obviously a fan of all things Egyptian, this woman did not *look* feeble-minded. Rather, she had an air of being in complete control. Her eyes, an unusual slate gray, stared into mine.

"Amisihathor was a songstress in the temple of Hathor. She sang to give pleasure to the goddess, and also at special ceremonies. It was an honored position, and she was proud of it. Her tomb is decorated with scenes of her duties, including a depiction of the Union with the Sun's disc at Wet-Renpet, a beautiful picture."

Well, even if the old woman was nuts, she knew her Egyptian history. The ancient New Year, Wet-Renpet, had begun in August, when the star Sirius reappeared, heralding the rising of the Nile. It was a time of rebirth and celebration, as the land was irrigated for crops. A special ceremony took place at Hathor's temple in Dendera. A gold statue of the mother goddess was carried onto a rooftop chapel, so that the sun could reinvigorate her with its light.

"Amisihathor's husband, Kahotep, was a powerful priest of Horus," the woman continued. "Most of the decoration on the walls of their tomb portray them performing rites, and having places of favor among the gods. The couple is the picture of marital bliss, of course. It was important to show the ideal, so that it could come true in the next world. But appearances can be deceiving."

"Really?" I asked.

She didn't seem to be put off by my tepid response. Instead, she continued as if I hadn't spoken. "I happen to know that Amisihathor, although buried alongside Kahotep and called his wife, was also married to a scribe from Edfu. Her name and images share the walls of *his* tomb, as well. And it was his declaration of love that she carried with her into the grave."

That *was* interesting. "What was it?"

"A letter. It was written on a scrap of papyrus and worn in an amulet around her neck. It addresses her as wife and is signed 'Kamenwati.' Either Kahotep was very open-minded, or he did not know what the amulet contained.

"I've done a great deal of research over the years. There was another oddity besides the letter. All the depictions of Amisihathor in the tomb of Kahotep were done hastily, as if it was not originally intended to include her. Of course, they could have been recently married, and just ran out of time. She was young when she died. But the more I discovered, the more the mystery deepened. There are references in the temple records to Amisihathor and a scribe from Edfu. Also, a letter written to Kahotep the month Amisihathor died, making mention of the fact that he had no wife. I suspected that Amisihathor did not belong in his tomb with him. But there was no proof until the scribe's tomb was discovered last year. You must have read about it?"

"Yes." The beautiful paintings had certainly caught my attention. "It had that lovely mural of his wife and him sitting under a palm tree, watching monkeys dance."

"Yes, indeed. Kamenwati, and Amisihathor. I knew it was the same woman. Egyptian art is very stylized, of course, but she had a unique piece of jewelry that was so beautiful, the artists included it in their representations. A necklace of turquoise and carnelian, with pearls and enameled lotus blossoms."

"The symbols of resurrection," I said automatically.

"Quite right." The old woman smiled. "You sign your paintings with one. The blue water lily."

"You've seen my work?" I asked in surprise.

"Of course. That was how I knew you were the one I needed to help me. We must unravel this mystery once and for all, so the spirits can go at last into the Beautiful West and find peace."

To my astonishment, she handed me a manila envelope.

"I've made copies of various inscriptions and documents, as well as an outline. We can talk again after you've read them. I'm certain you'll be intrigued. I've included my card, so you can call me anytime. Promise me that you'll go over it, Lily. It really is vital."

She rose before I could collect myself enough for a reply. "When you come to visit, I'll show you her necklace. Goodbye for now."

With incredible quickness for someone her age, she moved away into the crowd.

Chapter Two

I stood up, looking around anxiously. There was no sign of her, even after I had walked about searching. I had the idea that I ought to report her to someone. She was not fit to be out alone. What if she had given me something important?

I was about to go and notify security when I heard a voice say, "Excuse me." I looked up, and then further up. He was a very tall man. I knew what was coming as soon as I saw his eyes. They were the same odd, compelling shade of gray as the old woman's. His accent was English, too. "This is terribly awkward, but I believe you have something of my grandmother's?"

His tone was not accusing, but I turned red in embarrassment. The best defense is a good offense. "I've been looking for her," I said. "She disappeared while we were talking. I'm glad to see that she's not on her own."

He smiled slightly at the implied rebuke. "As you've discovered, she's not easy to keep track of. Not when she has her own plans. She's quite independent, is Gram."

"I hope she's all right now?" I inquired. I didn't see her anywhere near.

"She's with my brother in the foyer, feeling very pleased with herself. She told us that she'd found a new assistant. I gather she gave you some of her research?"

I waved the envelope. "If that's what this is. She seems to think I can help her in some way. My name is Lily Evans. I work for a professor of Egyptology at the University. Your grandmother has heard of me."

It sounded pompous after I'd said it, but the young man didn't appear to notice. "Ah, that explains it," he murmured. "Well, Miss Evans, I hope that Gram wasn't too intense for you. She lives and breathes ancient Egypt, and sometimes, she gets a bit carried away."

I liked the fact that he didn't say, "She's mad as a hatter," in his cultured British voice. I appreciated some family feeling. "She certainly knows her history," I said kindly.

He looked at me in bemusement. "Did she tell you who she was?" he asked.

"Uh, no. We never got that far. She was telling me about Amisihathor. She—has a theory about her. She must think I'm some kind of authority, but really, I'm not in a position…"

"It's all right," he assured me with a sudden smile. "There's no need to feel responsible."

"I'm only a research assistant. I haven't gotten my Ph.D. yet. Why don't you give these papers back to your grandmother, and tell her she can find someone better to help her."

That charming smile again. "You're a nice person, Lily Evans. Why don't you come along and let me formally introduce you? We'll get this straightened out."

Once again, I could have turned away. But I didn't. I found myself *wanting* to be formally introduced—to him. The night had taken a definite turn for the surreal. I was walking past mummies, following a dark, handsome stranger, to return mysterious papers to a woman who believed in ancient spirits. Not that my life was normally dull, but it definitely was not full of such stuff as this.

"What will your Ph.D. be in?" Handsome asked, as we made our way through the crowd.

"Ancient Egyptian studies. I specialize in art. I do drawings and paintings of life in ancient times."

"Really?" He sounded genuinely interested. "I'd like to see them sometime. Here we are."

We had arrived at the foyer, and I saw his grandmother on the arm of a man who was older, plumper, and lighter in coloring than my escort. Still, it was obvious that they were related. He nodded at me politely, and the old woman smiled in greeting. "How nice, Lily. Are you coming back with us tonight?"

"No, Gram," said my handsome stranger, patiently. "She doesn't even know who you are. You didn't tell her."

"No? I'm sorry, my dear. What must you think of me? I—"

7

But at that moment, a man who looked remarkably like Luciano Pavarotti came bustling up to our little group. "Dame Ursula!" he cried in a booming voice. "You're not leaving already?"

"I'm afraid so," was the quiet reply. "I'm feeling rather tired, John. You understand."

"Of course, of course. You and the boys must come and have dinner with us one night this week. Sandra will call and arrange it. All right?"

"Thank you. We'd be delighted. John, this is Lily Evans. She works at the University. Lily, John Costanza is the chief trustee on the museum board. His help has been invaluable in mounting this exhibition."

"Pleased to meet you," I stated, trying to control my amazement.

My outstretched hand was engulfed. "Miss Evans. I hope you enjoyed yourself? Did it meet your expectations?"

"Mr. Costanza," I said honestly, "I never imagined anything as exciting as this."

He beamed at me. "Wonderful! We were very lucky to get a collection of this caliber. I can't thank Dame Ursula enough. But I won't keep you any longer. Goodnight to you all!"

I turned my eyes from his retreating figure to my previously unknown companions. "You're Dame Ursula Allingham," I said deliberately. "The archaeologist. You discovered this tomb."

She smiled, as if I was a particularly clever student. "That's right. And these are my grandsons, Philip and Kent Ashton."

"I'm Kent," said my dark stranger. "Phil, would you take Gram out to the car while I say goodnight to Miss Evans?"

"Of course. Are you ready, Gram?"

"Indeed. I have done all that I wished. I'll see you again, Lily."

"It's been an honor, Dame Ursula. Thank you."

"Thank *you,* my dear."

And she was gone, leaving Kent and me alone together again.

"So," he said, "you've heard of my grandmother."

I took it for a rhetorical question, but replied anyway. "I'm an Egyptologist, Mr. Ashton. Of course I've heard of her. The tomb of Amisihathor was an important discovery. And my mentor, Professor Briggs, was a student of hers at Oxford."

"Yes. That's probably why Gram approached you."

"But why doesn't she just ask him for help? He's an expert," I protested.

"I'm afraid I don't know. May I look in the envelope as well?"

I tore it open. On the top was a page labeled 'The Excavation.' It was followed by several more pieces of paper, neatly typed, and illustrated with photo reprints and black and white drawings. From merely glancing through it, I could see it was a treasure trove of information.

"This is incredible," I breathed. "Your grandmother should write a book. I don't know what she thinks I could possibly add."

Kent didn't seem to know either, but he was too tactful to say so. "She must sense a kindred spirit," he said, simply.

"Or maybe she just enjoys my paintings. She's seen some of my work." I studied the end of the treatise Ursula had given me. "She's invited me to come over and discuss it with her. Please, Kent, tell her I'm very flattered, but explain that I'm just not qualified."

"I think you may be selling yourself short," Kent announced unexpectedly. "Gram is a good judge of talent. But I understand that you don't want to make a commitment. I'll tell you what. You look over this information. She'll be disappointed if you don't, and it will be interesting for you. Then we can have dinner next week and discuss it. I'd love to see some of your work. It would make a wonderful birthday present for Gram."

It might have been a strange situation, but no artist passes up the chance for a sale. Especially to a Dame's grandson. The fact that Kent was a very good-looking man may have influenced me too. But I didn't throw all caution to the wind. "If I can have your number, I'll check my schedule and let you know," I replied.

"Fair enough." He scribbled on a scrap of paper from his pocket. "Here's my mobile. If I don't answer, just leave a message." He pressed the information into my hand. "I hope I hear from you, Lily," he said. Really, those were extraordinary eyes. I dragged my gaze away from them.

"It was nice to meet you," I said. "Goodnight."

I turned back into the museum after he had gone, but didn't stay much longer. The exhibit seemed anti-climactic now. In a kind of daze, I went out to my car. When I started it up and switched on the radio, 'Walk Like an Egyptian' came warbling out at me. I laughed out loud and drove the twenty minutes to my home. I rented some rooms in a huge old Victorian house. My pet, Cleocatra, was waiting for me as I entered. She swished her long tail as if to ask how the evening had gone. "You wouldn't believe it," I said, as I bent down to stroke her back. I gave her a treat, then headed straight to the computer. I had some research to do on Dame Ursula Allingham.

Chapter Three

"Lily!"

I started as my friend, Katy, dropped a heavy volume of medieval history on my desk. The thud of the book, and the irritation in her voice brought me out of my reverie.

"What?" I asked. "Is the coffee maker broken again?"

This was usually the cause of bad temper in the otherwise affable Katy. But this time, her hostility was directed at me.

"*When* are you going to tell me what happened last night? You've been mooning around all morning, torturing me with wild hints about mummies and handsome English lords. I want details, and I want them *now!*"

"I promised I'd fill you in at lunch," I defended myself. "I have to finish verifying these quotations for Briggs…"

"Baloney," said Katy. "You're not working, unless staring into space constitutes work. So spill it, and maybe then you can concentrate."

She was right. I hadn't gotten very far with the information that Dr. Briggs needed for his latest paper, and he could be an impatient man. Being a research assistant to a noted Egyptologist was a job I loved, but today, it could not hold my interest, no matter what the work. The events of the night before seemed to be taking up all of the room in my brain. I decided that Katy was right, and I needed to tell my story.

"All right," I said, giving in. "But open up that book of yours, and pretend we're consulting if he comes by."

"Okay. I need to know about Egypt's influence on Richard the Lionheart. Now, come on!"

Katy had pulled up a chair and was looking at me expectantly. "Well," I began. "First of all, he's not a lord. Ursula's title is honorary, given for her services to archaeology. She's a Dame of the British Empire."

"Oh." Katy seemed a trifle disappointed. "But he *is* handsome?"

Kent's finely boned face and extraordinary eyes rose in my mind. "He certainly is," I answered. "And tall and dark!"

"So we have a storybook couple. Delicate little Lily and tall, strapping Kent. I do hope the children have your coloring. It would be a crime not to pass on those big brown eyes and perfect skin."

I ignored her prattling. "And he's so nice. Polite, but not in a smarmy way. Very genuine."

"Uh-huh." Apparently this was not high on the list of what Katy considered virtues. "And his grandmother found this mummy herself?"

"Yes. She and her husband were digging in Egypt in the 1950s, and excavated the tomb of Amisihathor, a priestess of Hathor. Hathor was the goddess of love and beauty, and also one of the chief funerary deities. She was worshipped throughout Egyptian history. There were some lovely objects buried with her that, unusually, hadn't been plundered. Both mummies were intact, too. Her husband was interred with her. He was a priest at the same temple, and the tomb was actually built for him. It was an important find, and Dame Ursula is well-respected."

"Did you find any hints about insanity?" asked Katy.

"Not a word. But I don't suppose it's the kind of thing they normally mention in scholarly articles. Anyway, she's come up with this theory that Amisihathor's spirit is not at rest. Dame Ursula wants me to help it reach the Beautiful West."

"California?" asked Katy flippantly.

"Your ignorance appalls me," I said with mock severity. "The Beautiful West was the Egyptian Paradise. Also called the Field of Reeds. You couldn't be at peace unless you got there. That's why they had such elaborate preparations. The Book of the Dead is full of the spells you needed to reach it. If you couldn't get past the demons and through the right gates of the Underworld, you never came before Osiris to be judged. That meant you had no chance of being found worthy to go on to paradise."

"Hard luck! And what exactly are you supposed to do to help this Amis—Amy—"

Katy hesitated over the strange name.

"Ah-me-see-hath-or." I spelled it out for her. "And the answer to your question is, I don't know. Ursula and I didn't get that far. She handed me an envelope full of documents, and then disappeared. While I was looking for her, Kent found me."

"And that's where the story *really* begins!" Katy grinned.

"It would be nice to sell a picture," I mused. "There's only been the one lately. I hope he meant it when he said he'd like to see some."

"Well, you'll find out when you call him, won't you? When are you planning on doing that? Tonight?"

"Maybe," I said, sidestepping her challenge. "Right now, I actually have to do some work. My art alone isn't going to support me!"

"Okay," Katy said obligingly, rising from her seat. "But you haven't been out on a date in a while. Don't think for one minute that I'm going to let you pass up a chance like this!"

She was as good as her word, and nagged me for the rest of the day. Finally, at four thirty, I gave in. Somehow, calling from work was easier. I composed a few different messages in my head, scolded myself mentally for going to so much trouble, and decided to just speak right off the cuff. Of course, as soon as I heard the voice at the other end of the line, my mind went completely blank.

"Hello?" said Kent, for the second time.

"Kent. Hi." I really hadn't expected him to answer in person, and I couldn't come up with anything more scintillating than that. But the warmth of his reply banished my reservations.

"Lily? I'm so pleased you called. How are you?"

I turned deliberately away from Katy, who was watching with unashamed interest. "I'm fine, thanks. And how is your grandmother doing?"

"As right as rain. She really enjoyed talking to you last night. I do hope you're going to let me take you out for dinner."

"That would be nice," I said demurely.

"Which evening is good for you?"

Why not throw all caution to the winds? "How about tonight?" I asked.

"Lovely. I'll let you choose the restaurant. Just ring and let me know the time and place. And bring some of your drawings with you. Will that be all right?"

"Sure. I'll see you later, then."

"Right. 'Bye, Lily."

Katy gave me the thumbs up sign as I replaced the telephone. "Good for you!" she said.

I had some doubt. "I hope he's not just being kind. He might feel guilty because he thinks his grandmother bothered me."

"Who cares!" Katy dismissed my qualms with a wave of her hand. "It doesn't matter what his motives are. You'll both have a great time, and if he buys a picture, so much the better!"

I couldn't argue with that. The studio displaying my work brought in some extra income, but it was erratic. A ready-made customer like Kent was manna from heaven.

"You're right, Katy. There's no downside, is there? Unless I fall madly in love with him, and he goes back to England and breaks my heart."

"That's the spirit!" Katy rolled her eyes. "Nothing like getting ahead of yourself. Just have a nice evening, show off your art, and enjoy the adventure. All right?"

"Yes, Katy," I said meekly.

Chapter Four

"Sometimes," said Kent, "I feel like I'm just going round and round in circles."

I smiled at him as he bobbed along beside me. "Just make sure not to change horses in midstream," I replied.

"Mommy, Mommy, look!" A small child ahead of us was shrieking in delight, waving maniacally as we passed her smiling parent. Lights glared, music blared, and I had seldom been so happy in my entire life.

I could hardly believe it when Kent had gotten on the carousel with me. Walking through the park after dinner, I had cast a wistful eye on the gaily-colored animals. "I loved riding that when I was a little girl," I had told him. "My father would bring me here a lot. At first, I sat in his lap in one of the swan seats. Then I graduated to a frog, and at last to the big horses. The first time he didn't have to stand beside me, I felt as if I was queen of the world. Not even driving gave me the same thrill."

"I've never seen so many different animals before," said Kent. "How old is it?"

"It's from 1911, and this is its original site. There used to be a huge amusement park here on the beach at the turn of the century. 'The Coney Island of Upstate', they called it. Only the carousel and the bathhouses are left now. Well, and the beach, of course."

"Brilliant!" said Kent. "Let's take a ride!"

"Really?"

"Yeah, really! If you can face public ignominy, that is," he teased.

"We'll sit right behind some children and maybe people will think we belong to them," I laughed.

"Right then, all aboard!" He took my hand and we climbed up on the wooden platform. "What's your fancy, my Lady? A carriage, or a steed?"

"I've always liked the brown horses best. They look friendlier, don't they?"

"Good choice. That leaves me the white stallion. I only hope I can keep him under rein." We got on, and as I put my feet in the stirrups, I was overwhelmed by a sense of déjà vu. It was a wonderful feeling.

I looked at Kent as the carousel spun around. He may not have been wearing armor, but he was a knight on a white horse all right. Even as I laughed at the symbolism, I felt a strange knot of emotion in my throat. I knew that I was falling in love with him. I had begun to suspect during dinner, where conversation was remarkably easy, and his quirky charm was captivating. But now, seated beside him on a merry-go-round, I was certain. And I could almost see my father smiling his approval.

I had told Kent how my father died when I was only ten. But I hadn't told him how much I missed him. Until tonight, I hadn't even considered the lack of a strong male presence in my life. My mother and two aunts were my only near relatives. I didn't have any close male friends, and only one boyfriend had really ever meant anything to me. It didn't matter that I had just met Kent. I felt that I could have him around forever.

He loved my drawings, as well. I could tell his appreciation was genuine. He hadn't been so crass as to purchase some and then take me out. He'd simply asked me to set aside two or three for later. It was understood that there were no obligations.

We hadn't discussed his grandmother except as background information. Kent seemed to adore her, hardly surprising since his parents had traveled extensively and Ursula had filled in as his surrogate mother. Her influence had helped, but it was his hard work and talent that had gotten him a job at the British Museum. "Stayed away from Egypt, though," he had informed me. "Family's still getting over that disgrace. First archaeologist in three generations not to get wrapped up in mummies. Etruscan Italy is my love. Fascinating civilization. I'll tell you all about it sometime, if you don't run fast enough."

His way of talking was like that, full of bad puns and light-hearted self-deprecation. We laughed a good deal. I was extremely comfortable with him. There was no first-date nervousness, a rarity for me. It was as if I'd known him for years. I ruthlessly silenced the little voice in my head that told me, "Don't be crazy. He'll be gone soon, back to London and out of your life." I did not want to think about that. I wanted to revel in the exhilaration coursing through me, and so far, I was succeeding.

When the carousel stopped, we hopped off and made our way to the custard stand. Kent was intrigued that you could get it frozen like ice cream. "It's a regional specialty," I said. "Like white hots and chicken wings."

"You Yanks eat such odd things! Aren't there any stands that sell normal food, like treacle tarts or blood pudding?"

"I can't imagine why, but no."

Kent sighed. "Well, give us one of these cones, then. I'll take a chance that it won't kill me."

"I'm proud of you," I said. "When in Rome…"

"Be sure to visit the Etruscan collection at the museum!" Kent finished.

We strolled along the pier as we ate our custard. Darkness had fallen and the lighthouse beacon was flashing. We stood listening to the water slap against the wood and the sound of boat engines humming towards shore. "I've had a lovely evening, Lily," Kent declared. "At the risk of being totally overbearing, would you like to do it again?"

Oh, would I! "When were you thinking of?" I asked.

"Tomorrow night? I know it's short notice, but…"

But I don't have a lot of time. The unspoken words hovered between us. "All right. I think I can manage that."

He looked as happy as I felt. "Lovely. Perhaps you can introduce me to more of these strange local customs."

"We could go to a baseball game and have popcorn and cotton candy and peanuts," I suggested.

"Cotton—oh, you mean candy floss," supplied Kent. "And drink *cold* beer? I don't think so. Football—sorry, soccer to you—is more my speed. I'm a diehard Sheffield Wednesday supporter. How about you?"

"The only thing I know about soccer is David Beckham. Is Sheffield Wednesday the name of a team or a player?"

He shook his head in mock disgust. "A team, of course, you lovely little Philistine. What do they teach you in these American schools?"

A sudden wind gusted off the lake and whipped my hair across my face. "Careful," Kent said. "You don't want hair-flavored custard." And he reached out and brushed back the strands gently. I exulted in the touch of his fingers against my cheek. It was such a tender gesture that my heart trembled. The little smile he gave told me that I was not alone in this mysterious madness. I closed my eyes as his lips met mine. I don't know how long we would have stood there in our own private world if a loud explosion hadn't rent the air. Some children screamed happily, and a flash of color streaked across the sky. "Fireworks!" I exclaimed.

Sure enough, a display was starting. I had forgotten that they were part of the harbor festival, and I blessed my decision to come here. It was the perfect ending to the most romantic date I'd ever been on. Such simple pleasures had turned out to be utterly unforgettable. I felt like I was walking in a dream, especially when Kent took my hand in his. We watched as the lights burst with brilliance, and sparks trailed down into the water. Katy was right. I decided to savor every moment of the present, and let the future take care of itself.

Chapter Five

Now, when I awoke in the mornings, I actually jumped out of bed. Cleocatra was clearly unsettled by my new enthusiasm. *What's going on?* she seemed to ask as she was shunted aside. I answered her yowl as if she had spoken the words. "I'm seeing Kent again today, Cleo. Isn't it wonderful?"

She invariably stalked away into the kitchen, letting me know that the only wonderful thing was breakfast. I hummed as I fixed it for her, daydreaming pleasantly. Kent and I had been out four times in the past week, and with each date, I felt closer to him. Ordinary events like a soccer game or a movie took on a magical quality. I would have been happy just sitting with him and watching the grass grow. It was exciting to be swept off my feet, and I kept myself from thinking of the time that they must touch the ground again.

This morning, I was pouring cereal into a bowl when the telephone rang. I knew who it was. Only my mother called so early, and besides, she had the uncanny ability to interrupt a meal. I put the box down and answered.

"Lily, is that you?"

There was no one else it could be, but for some reason she always asked. I said patiently, "Yes, Mom. How are you?"

"Oh, all right." The implication was that there were dire maladies she was choosing not to speak about. "And you?"

"I'm fine. As a matter of fact, I—"

"That's nice, dear. You will never guess who I talked to last night."

I could not let her get away with cutting me off this time. "Was it someone more interesting than Kent?" I asked. "Because, I've got to tell you, Mom, I—"

She went on as if I hadn't spoken. "Stephen!" she said triumphantly. "What do you think of that?"

I was too surprised to think anything. This was definitely a bolt from the blue. "Stephen Mallory? What did he want?"

"To talk to you, of course. He's back in town and he didn't have your new number. I expect you'll be hearing from him soon."

I felt a surge of aggravation. "Mom, I wish you would ask me before you just give that out. What if I don't *want* to talk to him?"

She sounded genuinely surprised. "But it's Stephen! I thought you'd be pleased."

A year ago, it would have been the most important thing in my life. But time had served to ease the memory of my ex-fiancé. He had gone out west to do his residency after medical school, but that was just the final nail in the coffin. Such a demanding career had left him little time for me. Once he left, I heard from him less and less until finally, communication had ceased altogether. It was a bit shocking to me that the mention of his name would still cause this knot of emotion.

"It would have been nice to know. Talking with him could be awkward. But I suppose I'll have to now. What did he say, exactly?"

"He was very sweet," my mother said defensively. "We just chatted for a minute. He told me how he missed New York and the change of seasons, and that Arizona wasn't what he was expecting. I think he wants to transfer to the hospital here. And he asked me for my oatmeal cookie recipe. He said he'd never found any even half as good."

This was a totally unexpected turn of events, and I was not ready to digest it.

"Well, we'll see what happens," I said non-committally. "Right now, Kent is taking up all of my time. He is so special, Mom. I really want you to meet him."

"It's hard to believe that there's anyone as special as Stephen. He wouldn't be here unless he still had feelings for you. At least talk to him, Lily."

I had had enough of this conversation. "I'm sorry Mom, I've got to go. My cereal is getting soggy. I'll call you later, okay?"

I hung up feeling disgruntled. My mother had always been fond of Stephen, and had never recovered from losing the chance of having a doctor as a son-in-law. He hadn't exactly broken up with me, to be fair. More just sort of moved on. I hadn't been willing to leave the university, or go to Arizona and sit alone while he worked endless intern's hours. Still, I had loved him, and his loss had been very painful for me.

How strange that he should be coming back.

It nagged at me as I ran errands and cleaned the apartment, but as the afternoon passed, any stray thought of Stephen was banished from my mind. Kent had agreed to pick me up at three o'clock, and I couldn't wait to see him.

Our destination that afternoon was Sunny Hill, a lavish Victorian estate now open to the public. The mansion was preserved in keeping with the period, and it was surrounded by twenty-seven acres of magnificent gardens. Each one had its own theme, and I felt a glow of pride when Kent was impressed. "It's as beautiful as any I've seen at home," he declared. We made our way leisurely through them all. I had visited the place many times, but it came alive for me in a new way as I showed it off to Kent. The flowers seemed to have more color, the follies were more picturesque, the miniature temples and hidden grottos more impossibly romantic. We ate dinner in the outdoor café, and then went to the last attraction. It was my favorite, the Japanese Garden. We strolled along the stone path, over the little humpbacked bridge, and up to the red teahouse. Together, we sat down on a large flat boulder in front of it. Dragonflies went shimmering by, catching the late sun on their wings. Carp swam lazily in the ponds surrounding us. I was imagining all this being mine, when Kent said, "It would be brilliant, wouldn't it?"

We were so much in sync that I wasn't even surprised at this apparent reading of my thoughts. "I'd change a few things," I remarked. "The Italian garden is too formal for me. I'd plant lilacs and rhododendrons instead."

"I'd have fewer statues. You don't want them looking at you all the time."

"The one of Diana in the little Greek temple can stay, though. I like that."

"Fine. I grant you Diana. But that chap wrestling with the fish goes."

I laughed. "That's Hercules slaying the Hydra," I informed him.

"It's ghastly is what it is. I don't care for the Four Seasons in the Sub Rosa either. You can tell that Winter is just waiting for you to turn your back."

"Were you afraid of the nightingale in the Moonlight Garden?" I inquired.

"Ah, well, they're a rough lot, nightingales. They charm you with their singing, and as soon as your guard's down, they fly straight for your jugular."

"I had no idea! They seem so harmless. We'd better not have any statues, to be on the safe side." How naturally this daydream had turned into 'ours.' That's how it was with Kent. If I had believed in reincarnation, I would have thought I'd known him in a previous life. The connection between us was so warm and real.

"No statues," he agreed. "But we want lots of roses. And a gazebo in the middle for whiling away the summer evenings."

Dusk would be falling soon on this summer evening. Reluctantly, I knew we would have to be going. "That sounds lovely," I replied. "But for now, they can still kick us out of here. We'd better head back."

Kent stood up and pulled me to my feet. Hand-in-hand, we made our way down a long avenue lined with bay trees. At the end, a huge pair of wrought-iron gates led into the parking lot. As we climbed into Kent's rented Camry, an early firefly flickered past in the gathering darkness. "When I was a little girl," I said, "my father told me that those were the lights of fairies. Sometimes, I can still half believe it."

There was no sarcastic reply from Kent. Instead, he remarked, "You mention your Dad a lot. He must have been very special."

"Oh, he was." And suddenly, I wanted to tell Kent all about him. The overwhelming love I had felt for him, the jealousy of my mother, the covert campaign to stop me from being such a 'daddy's girl.' I was made to go shopping and help bake cookies and participate in other feminine activities that I had no interest in. I wanted only to hang about the yard while he did the outdoor work, or go on walks where we would always find something fascinating: an oddly-shaped rock, a blue robin's egg, a fossil he would always assure me was at least a million years old. Memories poured out of me in torrents, and Kent listened to them all. He was so attentive that it made it natural and easy to share. I found myself verbalizing thoughts that until now had been only vague nameless fears in my mind. How, when my father had died, an awful guilt had possessed me, that it was because I had loved him too much. It must have been wrong, somehow. Kent answered with uncharacteristic grimness.

"If adults knew what ideas children got into their heads, they'd be a lot more careful. At least, one would hope so. I thought that if I were a more lovable boy, my parents wouldn't travel so much. Why else would they stay gone for so long? It could only be because Phillip and I weren't interesting enough to hold their attention. What burdens we carried around, love, without even knowing it. Guilt is the cruelest emotion, and the most useless. We felt like we'd committed a crime, but there was nothing we could do about it."

He put his arm around me and we sat there together, unmoving and silent, for several minutes. I felt intimately connected to him. The sense of closeness was so intense, it was almost painful. It was an emotional growth burst, as if something long dormant inside of me was now shaking off dirt and stretching up towards the sun. I sensed that it was no less powerful for Kent.

It was a security guard who broke the spell. He came to lock the gates, and Kent disengaged himself from me gently. "I think they want to be getting home. But the night is young for us. Why don't we visit your local and have a nosh?"

"Would you mind translating that into American?" I asked with a smile.

"Do you have a favorite club, bar, place where you go to drink and get food?"

"Yes, I do, and that's a great idea," I said.

"Let me just stop at the house on the way and check on a couple of things. Is that all right? Gram did express an interest in saying hello to you. I think she feels badly about the other night."

"I don't mind at all," I assured him. Secretly though, I couldn't help but wonder what his grandmother might come up with this time.

Chapter Six

Kent's family was staying at the home of the University's president, while he was traveling in Europe. It was a beautiful turn-of-the-century stone house, with a big wooden front door that reminded me of a drawbridge. A fitting residence for a prince, I thought whimsically.

Dame Ursula was sitting in the living room, and she greeted me with enthusiasm.

"What a pleasure to see you again, Lily! I trust my grandson is being good company?"

Kent smiled at me, and I was afraid that I was blushing. "Excellent company, thank you," I replied.

"I'm glad to hear it. I wonder if I might speak with you alone for a few minutes. I promise I won't intrude on your evening together for long."

I sensed Kent's discomfort, and hastened to say reassuringly, "Of course, Dame Ursula. I'd love to talk."

Kent began backing out of the room. "I'll just make a couple of phone calls, then."

"Fine, dear." Ursula waited until he had fully retreated, then sighed fondly. "Those boys are two of the best men in the world, and I adore them. But I don't believe they'd understand this particular problem."

"You haven't told them about the Amisihathor puzzle?" I queried.

"Well, no, not the whole story. They'd think that the Egyptian sun had addled my wits. You are the only person I am going to reveal the secret of the necklace to."

In spite of my trepidation, I was strangely touched. "I'm honored, Dame Ursula, but—"

"Please, there's no need to be formal, Ursula will do. And you're wondering why I've chosen to confide in you. It wasn't an arbitrary decision. I visited the local gallery the first day we came into town. I do that whenever we travel. Your paintings caught my eye right away. You have a great deal of talent. I asked several people about you, and they all sang your praises. Particularly Peter Briggs. He and I have known each other for a long time. He used to date my daughter, you know."

"Kent's mother?" I asked in surprise.

"That's right. Peter was a student of mine at Oxford. He and Cassandra became great friends. But then he returned here, to America, and Cassie married Kent's father. Her life was very different after that." Ursula sighed, then seemed to push a sad memory away. "We were very fond of Peter, and thrilled with his success. He speaks highly of you, Lily. He says you have a good mind, and I think you also have a good heart." She smiled at me. "Then there's your kinship for ancient Egypt. I recognize an insider's view. Tell me, do you have any Egyptian blood?"

"On my father's side," I replied. "But it's many generations back, and I've never been there. I simply love the culture. I always have."

Ursula nodded. "Physical and spiritual DNA. That's why you are able to draw the things you do. Like the scene in this painting."

To my surprise, she rose and went over to a heavy teak desk in the corner of the room. Opening a drawer, she produced one of my pictures.

"I purchased it as soon as I saw it. Tell me, what inspired you to do this particular design?"

It was one of my favorites. A garden surrounded by palm trees, with a pool in the middle. Lotus blossoms were floating on the water, and brightly colored fish swam among them. I could not remember any one thing that had made me draw it. It just seemed to be a place that existed in my dreams.

"I wonder," said Ursula, when I told her this, "if you've ever seen pictures of Amisihathor and Kahotep's tomb?"

"Some, of course. It was a very important find. I loved the chance to study them at the exhibit."

"Well, this scene is not included in the exhibit. There aren't any published photographs of it, as far as I know. Not outside of my own documentation. The paint is damaged, so it doesn't make for good copy. But it's on the west wall, after the depictions of her duties in the temple. You've drawn it down to the last detail. Even the turtle sunning itself on the rock is there."

I shook off an odd sense of unease. "I suppose I must have seen it, then," I said briskly, "and I just don't remember. I'm flattered that you liked it enough to buy it." This, then, was her reason for singling me out. An image that I'd stored in my subconscious and painted, which happened to be from Amisihathor's tomb. At least there was an element of logic in her fancy.

"I think you will be the one to discover what happened to Amisihathor, and put her soul at rest," Ursula stated.

She said this so reasonably, as if discussing my qualifications for an ordinary job. I answered in the same tone. "And how am I supposed to do that, Dame Ursula?"

"You already have a connection with Amisi. You proved that with your painting. I would like to look at all of your work, to see what else I may recognize. And then, of course, there's the necklace."

"You've mentioned it before," I said. "It *is* lovely, but what makes it so special?"

"It is an object of great power," Ursula asserted solemnly. "I believe it to be infused with psychic energy."

"What—like magic?" I asked incredulously.

"Magic." She repeated the word in a thoughtful way. "Some might call it that. But to the ancients, magic did not exist as a separate concept. It was a part of their religion, the way we say prayers and perform symbolic ceremonies. Nowadays, it's even come under the scrutiny of science. Studies are done on the power of faith in healing. The ways meditation and hypnosis affect your brain waves. The nature of consciousness. There are even instruments being used to measure ghostly phenomenon. Some researchers believe that we are all made up of living energy, which may change forms, but can never be destroyed. They say that we can leave an imprint of that energy in the atmosphere, or on certain objects. I admit, in the past, I would have found the notion ridiculous. But I have become more open-minded in my old age. The willingness to explore new ideas and look for evidence is how we develop knowledge, after all.

"Personal experience has convinced me that magic, religion, spirituality—whatever you want to call it—is a potent force. It unleashes tremendous energy, and that energy can take many forms. Some of it is left in Amisihathor's necklace. I only felt a trace of it, but I'm not very sensitive. I think that you will see more. Are you willing to look, Lily?"

I was silent for a moment, debating on how to answer her. At last, I said carefully, "Ursula, I'm not a medium. The painting was just a coincidence. I have no special gifts. The evidence you've gathered about the mystery surrounding Amisihathor is certainly intriguing, but I don't know how I can help you."

"You're not convinced that a magic necklace will give you answers?" Ursula replied mildly. "Don't worry. I am continuing traditional research as well. All I ask is to examine your artwork, and for *you* to examine the jewelry. That will not be a burden on you, will it?"

I was reluctant to turn her down flat. "Well, I would like to see it. I didn't notice it at the exhibit. I gather it's not on public display."

"Not yet. Some pieces will be rotated. I'll take you over and we'll have a private viewing. You'll enjoy that."

"I would," I replied truthfully. "Thank you, Ursula. And you're welcome to come and have a private viewing of my work also."

At that moment, Kent came back into the room. "Well, have you two solved the riddle of the Sphinx yet?" he teased.

His grandmother smiled at him. "One thing at a time, dear," she said sweetly. "Right now, we are discussing Amisihathor. Lily has agreed to help me with my research."

"Oh?" Kent's eyebrows lifted slightly.

"Yes, isn't that nice? I'm in need of a new perspective. Away with you two, now. I've monopolized Lily for long enough. We'll talk tomorrow and make arrangements, if that's all right?" she asked me.

"Of course. Thank you, Ursula," I said, rising to my feet. She gave me a pleased smile. "Goodnight. You children enjoy yourselves."

Kent kissed her on the cheek. "Goodnight, Gram. Sleep tight."

We went into the library and settled ourselves on the couch. Kent sat very close, and our knees touched pleasantly. "I thought perhaps I'd better come and see what was up," he said. "Was it all about Amisihathor?"

"Yes." I hesitated. "You know how Ursula's—preoccupied with her."

He nodded. "And it doesn't usually matter. It's her life's work. But she's never done anything like she did with you before."

"Well, there's a reason for that. She's convinced Amisihathor needs her help. I think she wants to reunite her with her true love in the afterlife."

"Her true love? You mean the scribe in the second tomb?"

"The same. She must believe they got seperated, and she wants to find out what happened to them."

"But the evidence is so fragmented, she may never be able to do that."

Now came the difficult part. Feeling a sense of responsibility, but an equal one of reluctance, I searched for the right words. "Actually, she has a backup plan. An alternative method, so to speak."

"Which would be...?" Kent prompted when I showed no sign of going on.

I cleared my throat. "She has an idea... she seems to think that... perhaps the necklace found in the tomb might be helpful."

"How, exactly?"

"Well—ah—do you believe in psychic energy, Kent?" I asked conversationally.

"What do you mean?" he questioned warily. "Like bending spoons with your mind?"

"More like fingerprints being left behind. The residue of your energy, your emotions, after you've gone. Sometimes, it lingers, and that's why places seem haunted. Places, or—things."

He stared at me, as if he was mentally measuring me for a straightjacket. "Are you telling me that the necklace is haunted?"

"No! I'm simply saying that Ursula believes it is."

"Oh, well, that's all right then," he said sarcastically.

"I know, it sounds crazy," I conceded. "But to Ursula, and a lot of other people, it makes sense. She thinks that it's possible to see the past in the necklace. At least, for me to see it."

"And where on Earth did she get that idea?" he asked distractedly.

I told him about my painting. "Once she saw it, and learned who I was, she became convinced that I could help her." I paused. "You haven't had any reason to think she's—well—troubled, have you?"

"I would have said 'no' before tonight," Kent replied morosely. "'Eccentric' is the word I've always used."

"Yes," I reflected. "She reminds me of my great-aunt Elizabeth. She used to talk to the ghost of Abraham Lincoln. He told her which horses to bet on at the track. Other than that, she was completely normal. Since she almost always won, the doctor said not to worry about it."

Kent merely gazed at me, and I suspected that this did not comfort him.

"Look," I said, "why don't you just keep an eye on her and see what you think. Maybe you can convince her to see her own doctor, have a checkup. Then you can discuss your concerns with him. But please don't let her know that I talked to you. This was supposed to be in confidence."

Kent sighed. After a while, he said, "Thank you, Lily. I'm sorry you had to get involved in this. It's wonderful of you to care. But please realize that you're under no obligation."

I could not tell him that I did indeed feel an obligation. Not just to Ursula, whom I liked tremendously, but to him. I felt a connection that I knew was dangerous on such a short acquaintance. However, the knowledge did nothing to lessen its intensity. I was caught up with this family, practical or not.

Chapter Seven

"Oh, man, this just keeps getting better and better!" said Katy gleefully. We were sitting in a bagel shop on Sunday morning, and I was filling her in on the weekend's events. "Let's see." She began ticking items off on her fingers. "A mysterious old woman. Ancient magic and restless spirits. A tall, dark and handsome stranger. English aristocracy. Money. Madness. What are we missing? Ah, danger. I don't suppose there was a deranged servant lurking around their house?"

"No, Katy. I didn't catch a glimpse of a Mrs. Danvers."

"Too bad. Well, maybe brother Philip will turn out to be a homicidal maniac. We can always hope."

"Sorry to burst your bubble, but Philip is a highly respectable businessman. His company makes dental equipment."

Katy pulled a face. "How awful! But never mind, the prestige of Kent's job more than makes up for that."

"He's very young to have such an important position at the British Museum," I said proudly.

"Good for him. You have hit the jackpot, haven't you? This makes a story you'll be able to look back on in your old age. Congratulations!"

"What? You're not going to tell me that I've gotten myself into a bizarre situation with people I barely know, and I had better be careful?"

"Why on Earth would I do that?" Katy lavished her bagel lovingly with cream cheese as she continued. "What you've got yourself is an adventure, and they don't come along every day. These aren't shadowy underworld figures. It's a well-known British family who shares an interest in the love of your life—ancient Egypt. You say that Kent is gorgeous and you really like him. Your boss could have been his father, for Pete's sake!" She grinned at her own pun. "So stop worrying! Even if he's gone in a couple of weeks and you never hear from him again, it will have been great while it lasted. You'll hardly pine after him for the rest of your life, not after so short a time. If you ask me, this is just what you need."

I couldn't help but laugh. "I can always count on you to be the voice of reason, Katy."

"At your service." Then she sobered. "Honestly though, Lily, you like this Dame Ursula? She doesn't give you the creeps?"

"No, she doesn't. It's not like she's a raving lunatic. There's a kind of logic in her scenario. It doesn't seem so strange to me that she would need to wrap up the work on the tomb in her own mind. The idea of the necklace having magic powers is a little odd, of course—"

"A little," Katy agreed equably.

"—But the Egyptians believed in magic, and Ursula has studied them for so long that it's not surprising she might believe now too. She's not threatening in any way, if that's what you mean."

"Okay. And you trust Kent?"

"Kent," I replied decisively, "is what the Brits term 'a thoroughly decent chap.' No worries there."

"Heaven help us, you're already beginning to talk like them!" mocked Katy. "Well, I say go with your instincts. If they seem all right, then they probably are. To reduce it to the crassest level: if nothing else, you've sold some of your paintings! It will get you noticed in wider circles. How can that hurt?"

It couldn't. But on one point, Katy was wrong. I already knew that I *would* pine for Kent, even after so short a time. Living in the moment was all very well, as long as that moment was not the one in which he left.

I took a sip of my iced tea and changed the subject. "You won't believe who's come to town," I said.

"Right now, I'd believe anything as far as you're concerned. A government official who wants you to be a spy? A long lost relative with a terrible secret? Maybe the heir to some throne, hiding from assassins?"

"Actually," I said, "it's Stephen. He called my Mom on Friday night. She got the idea that he wants to move back here, but I don't know if that's true. I haven't spoken to him yet."

Katy's animated face went uncharacteristically flat. "Oh, Stephen," she murmured. "I thought he was gone for good."

"It's all right," I said, humorously. "We've broken up, so you can let your true feelings show."

"You already know what I think of him." Katy stirred her coffee vigorously. "He was always a little too arrogant for my taste. What's he doing back here, anyway? Haven't they made him president of the AMA yet?"

"I'll be sure to give him your love when he calls," I grinned. Which turned out to be that very evening.

I had just come in from grocery shopping when the phone rang. Hoping that it was Kent, I snatched up the receiver. "Lily?" asked a familiar voice. "It's Stephen."

"Oh—hello! How are you, Stephen?"

"Fine. And you? It's been a long time."

A long time, and a lot of tears. It felt good to be able to tell him, truthfully, "I'm doing great. Yeah, it has been a while. Mom told me you were here in town."

"I just got back last week. I'm going to be working at Hope. I missed New York, you know? You don't realize it until you leave."

I refused to see any double meaning in his words. "I don't blame you," I said. "I love the change of seasons and all the different scenery we have. Hope's a great hospital. I'm sure you'll do well there."

"My old stomping grounds. It'll be nice to have a handle on everything."

Yes, that was what Stephen always wanted. "Well, congratulations on being a resident," I replied. "You worked so hard, and it's a tremendous accomplishment."

"Thanks, Lily. You of all people know how much I had to sacrifice. But when you see the difference you can make, it keeps you going. Last month, I assisted in a spinal operation on a six-year-old girl. I was there when she took the first steps of her life. Her mother was crying and took my hand to whisper, 'Thank you.' I had tears in my eyes too. It's hard to describe how that makes you feel."

"I'll bet." My admiration was sincere. "You're a wonderful doctor, Stephen."

"Enough about me. I want to hear what's happening with you. Will you come out and have a drink with me? I'd love to catch up."

Apparently, he felt no awkwardness about this situation, but I still did. "Well, I'm not sure when I'm free. Can I get back to you?"

"Of course. Got a pen? I'll give you my number."

I reflected as I wrote it down that I was bound to be running into him soon. The hospital adjoined the University, and it was not a big city. Perhaps it was best to get it over with. But I wasn't going to give up any time with Kent.

"Maybe we can meet one lunchtime. I'll let you know in the next couple of days," I said.

"Okay. It will be great to see you again, Lily. I'll talk to you soon."

Katy was right, I thought as I hung up. My life was getting to resemble a romantic novel of late. Here I had a brand-new love interest, and right on his heels, the old one was returning. But it's all over with Stephen, I reminded myself. From now on, we would meet only as friends, if indeed we managed that.

Cleocatra was rubbing against my ankles impatiently, waiting to see if I had brought her anything home from the store. "Yes, I remembered your treats," I told her. "Just wait a minute until I can get this stuff put away. Cleo, can you believe everything that's been happening lately?"

My pet meowed as if to say that she, like Katy, could believe anything.

Chapter Eight

I felt like a kid in a candy store as I stood in the basement of the museum. Acutely aware of the privilege being bestowed, I feasted my eyes on the artifacts in front of me. They were lying all about, not locked away behind glass cases, but right where I could touch them. Ursula was with me, providing a fascinating commentary.

"This is her cosmetic palette." Ursula showed me a wooden form in the shape of a duck. "Amisihathor mixed the pigments for her eye and cheek color in the grooves. And here," indicating a small alabaster jar, "she kept her perfume. These are some of her pins, and beads she wove into her hair. People don't change much through the years, do they? Always trying to look their best. I wish I could show you the oracular decree and the letter that she wore in her amulet, but they were so fragile that they had to be preserved and kept in Cairo. The copies I put into your folder."

I had read those. The decree was a spell that the Egyptians wore, protected in a cylindrical amulet. They were written on small pieces of papyrus, and represented promises from the gods. Amisihathor's was in the form of a blessing from Hathor:

'I grant unto my beloved servant, strength of limb and joy of heart. Daughter of eternity, she shall walk in a dream garden, knowing sweetness in this life and the next.'

The letter, written on a scrap of papyrus, was from the scribe Kamenwati. It told of his love for her, and how much she was missed. And yet she had been put to rest beside another man in another tomb with all of her possessions. It was certainly an intriguing mystery.

I examined the treasure trove raptly. At last, I came to the object for which all this had been arranged: Amisihathor's necklace. It was a collar strung with rows of beads, red carnelian alternating with blue turquoise and green feldspar. On either side were lotus blossoms enameled with lapis lazuli. These were connected by a row of pearls forming a clasp. Amisihathor—the flower of Hathor. And her flower was the lily.

"It's beautiful, isn't it?" asked Ursula gently. "We discovered so many wonderful items in the tomb, but when I found that, I knew it was special. It's difficult to describe what happened when I held it. I remember thinking of Amisihathor and how she must have touched it every day of her life. It brought her closer to me than anything else had done. I kept staring—I couldn't seem to tear my eyes away. And then I fancied that I saw another pair of eyes. They were wide and dark and filled with a terrible sadness. The pain hit me as if it were my own. I think I must have cried out, because the next thing I knew, my fellow workers were gathered around me. I was made to sit down and drink water, and I just went along with their notion that I was overworked. I didn't tell anyone what had happened—how could I? We stopped for that day, but the image stayed in my mind. I crept back to the dig very early, before anyone else was about, and held the necklace again. Again, I felt the sense of loss and sadness. And a name came into my head. 'Kamenwati.'"

"The scribe," I said.

"Yes. Only I didn't know that at the time. He was completely unfamiliar to me. But afterwards, I found two references to him in the temple records. The first notes that a scribe by that name had come from Edfu and joined the residents at the temple. The other announces the promotion of the scribe to a higher position in the priesthood at Dendera. 'Kamenwati and his wife, Amisihathor, rejoice and give thanks to the great lord Horus.' They probably performed some type of offering, and this is a reference to it. Excavations have gone on for years, but you know how painstaking they are. No more tantalizing information came my way until the discovery of Kamenwati's tomb. Then I was vindicated. There she was, Amisihathor herself, identified once again as a songstress of Hathor, beloved wife, but this time of an entirely different man!"

"The tomb wasn't finished, was it?" I asked. "They didn't find a mummy."

"Not even a sarcophagus. None of the decoration was complete. It looked as if work had just stopped. Kamenwati simply disappears. Excavations have continued in the area, but nothing else pertinent has turned up. I could do nothing but continue to search, and wait until the right person came along to help me. I'm certain that person is you, Lily. Please take the necklace and look at it with an open mind. If you feel Amisihathor's presence as I did, it will not be pleasant. Just remember that it is not *your* story. You are a spectator only, and there is no danger. I am going to leave you now in peace, but I'll be in the next room if you need me." And with that, she was gone.

I stood there for a minute, feeling a little ridiculous. At least Ursula was not breathing down my neck waiting for some kind of response. I could simply examine the artifact and let her know the truth: that it was fascinating and beautiful, but totally bereft of magical power.

But when I did pick it up, another sort of feeling came over me altogether. Like someone was walking over my grave. Or, rather, like I was walking over someone else's. I was surprised by the shudder that passed through me. Ursula had obviously gotten my imagination working overtime. Gingerly, I held the heavy chain in my gloved hands, gazing down at the intricate designs.

Nothing. I almost smiled in relief. I realized that a very small part of me had been expecting to see a dark, exotic face from the past. But of course, Amisihathor was three thousand years dead, and nothing remained of her in this necklace but a memory. I experienced a moment of sadness, thinking of her leaving the world so young, everything she knew and loved receding from her grasp. Then fear, the burning of frustrated emotions, the desperate desire to tell them ... tell *him*...

But it is too late! I am alone, all alone. Oh, my love, forgive me, I did not realize! Will I see you in the afterlife now? Will you take my hand and smile at me?

Beloved, be with me. Mistress, welcome me into the western mountain. Let maat prevail...

37

I gasped suddenly like a person released from drowning. I felt as if I had not breathed in ages. At first, I could think of nothing but getting enough air in my lungs. Then I put down the necklace and stumbled over to a nearby chair. I was so drained of energy that I was afraid I was going to faint. I put my head down between my knees, and, gradually, the sickness passed. Slowly, I sat up.

What had just happened to me? My mind was already finding reasons to push away the threat of the inexplicable. The past week had been a very emotional time. My life was undergoing considerable change. No wonder I was in such a suggestible state. Surrounded by ancient artifacts, primed by a famous archaeologist with dramatic theories, was it so unusual that my imagination would get the better of me? Of course not. Of *course* not, I repeated firmly, just to make sure my mind understood. And to further convince it, I reminded myself that I hadn't eaten anything since breakfast. Ursula had set this appointment up after museum hours, and I had been too excited to think about lunch or dinner. All of these factors had come together to cause a dizzy spell. Natural. Perfectly natural.

I waited until I felt normal again. Then, without another glance at the table, I went into the next room to find Ursula.

Her look of anticipation quickly changed to one of concern. "My dear, you're so pale! Are you all right?"

"Fine," I replied, in what I hoped was a calm tone. "I had a little dizzy spell, that's all. That's what happens when you skip two meals!"

Ursula looked at me steadily. "What did you see, Lily?" she asked.

I did not want to encourage her fantasies. But I did not want to lie, either. "I didn't *see* anything," I answered cautiously. "I do understand what you experienced, though. It's easy to imagine how it would feel to be facing death, thinking about your loved ones, wondering what was going to happen. It's a very powerful, moving..." My words trailed off, knowing I could never do justice to the impact of those emotions. But Ursula seemed completely satisfied with my response.

"All right, dear. You don't have to say anymore now. I'm sure this day has been quite long enough for you. You go and eat something and have a nice, relaxing evening. Are you certain you're well enough to drive? I'll be happy to have Philip drop you off."

I was anxious to get home and do as she said, so I assured her that I was fine. Truthfully though, I still felt exhausted and on edge. When I did reach my apartment, I collapsed on the bed gratefully. I was supposed to call Kent and tell him what had happened, but found the prospect too fatiguing. In a little while, I thought, as I closed my eyes. I remembered the strange words that had gone through my head as I held the necklace of Amisihathor. *Beloved, be with me. Let maat prevail.* Maat, the ancient Egyptian concept of order and right. It was against a feather from the goddess Maat's headdress that a heart was weighed on the day of judgment. If it was heavy with sin, one could not go on to the afterlife. A dreadful beast, Ammit the Destroyer, waited to devour the wicked. It was essential to have truth on one's side. What was the truth concerning Amisihathor?

Cleocatra jumped up next to me, gave a soft hiss, and jumped back down. In the cool stillness, it was not long before I was asleep.

Chapter Nine

The Golden One has come to visit with her husband, the wise and mighty Horus. She sits in the sacred barque, in the courtyard of the god's house. The air crackles with excitement. It is a joyous time, and everyone is celebrating. I sing the goddess' praises with great pride. Dancers and musicians perform in her honor. We are a large, boisterous crowd, for many people have joined our procession along the way. For days, we have traveled from Dendera, down the Nile, to reach this shining temple. Tonight, the gods will rejoice in the marriage bed, and for two weeks, we shall stay in this place while the festival lasts. This is the first time I have taken part in the Feast of the Beautiful Reunion. All the sights, sounds, and smells thrill me. An acrobat tumbles past, the bells on his ankles tinkling. Two dwarves follow him, shaking tambourines. A servant of Horus is handing out honey cakes. I suddenly realize that I am yearning for food and drink. As if the gods hear me, there is a voice at my elbow. "A cup of wine, mistress? Your sweet singing must be making your throat dry."

I turn my head, and my eyes blink. Is it the bright sun, or the smile on the face of the man before me? I accept the vessel from his hand. "Many thanks," I say. "Your offer is well-timed."

"I am pleased, lady of Hathor." He glances at my nearby companions. "Perhaps you would like to sit in the shade for a few moments? I know of a spot, by the wall. There is a palm tree that gives protection."

It would be good to rest awhile, I muse. But in my heart, I know that is not truly the reason I wish to accompany him.

"You are most gracious. Let me tell my sisters, and I will come with you."

No one else wants to leave the hub of activity. Merety, the most senior of our group, looks at the young man with an air of appraisal. "A well-favored lad, to be sure! A scribe in the house of Horus, I see by his badge. Go, Amisihathor, but do not be long. The races will be starting soon."

With only my maid, Tia, trailing along behind me, I return the short distance to where he waits. We begin walking together towards the high stone walls surrounding the temple. "I am Kamenwati, a servant in the House of Life," he tells me. "You have come with the goddess from Dendera?"

"Yes. My name is Amisihathor, and I am a chantress of Hathor. This is my first trip to Edfu."

"And how do you find it so far?" he asks attentively.

"Wonderful! There is so much to see and do, I scarcely know where to look next!"

He laughs pleasantly at my enthusiasm. "Yes, it is exciting. There are more people here than ever before. I have seen with my own eyes men who have come from the land of Punt. What do you think they had with them? Monkeys! Monkeys on golden chains, as tame as any dog. By Ra, I swear it. They ate figs and chattered away like children!"

My eyes grow wide with wonder. "I should dearly love to witness that!"

"Perhaps you shall, my lady. If you would prefer to walk about with me, rather than resting, we will look for them."

I nod eagerly. Any tiredness has vanished.

"Very well! But you had better stay close to me in these crowds. May I take your hand?"

I hold it out shyly, and Kamenwati closes his fingers around mine. I feel a little shiver go up my spine. His grasp is warm and strong. Suddenly, I feel as if nothing can threaten me. I am heady with a sense of adventure. We weave our way among the masses while Tia strives to keep up. The scent of incense from all the offerings is strong on the air. Kamenwati points out different travelers and tells me where they are from. His knowledge, like everything else about him, impresses me. He stops to procure cakes and bread for us to eat, and presents me with a fresh garland of flowers. His fingers brush against my neck as he drapes it over me. Our eyes meet and hold. If all the monkeys in Punt should pass by at this moment, I would not spare them a glance. For I am looking at the most magical and marvelous sight the gods have ever invented. I am looking into the face of the man I love.

"Mistress!"

Tia's voice is at my ear like the buzz of an unwelcome insect. "Mistress, we must be returning to the group now. The priestess herself instructed us to be back for the races!"

I want to ignore her, but I cannot. I must do my duty. Reluctantly, I say to Kamenwati, "I'm afraid I have to be going. I have had a wonderful time. Thank you."

"Of course. There are rituals to be performed. But we will meet again." He gives a little bow. "I will make sure of it."

He escorts us back to where the elders of my temple are gathered. As we say goodbye, he leans over and whispers to me. "I will come to this same spot tomorrow. Until then, farewell, beautiful lady."

A screech rent the air, and I was suddenly sitting bolt upright in bed. My cat was batting at my head with her paw, and when I glanced at the clock, I understood why she was acting impatient. It was almost nine-thirty, and her dinner was long overdue. So, I thought ruefully, was my phone call to Kent.

I got up and filled Cleo's bowl, giving her extra to atone for my neglect. Then I checked my messages. Ursula had called to see how I was feeling, and Kent had rung twice. I dialed his cell number right away.

"At last!" he said when he answered. "I was worried. Gram told me you had some kind of dizzy spell. What happened?"

"I just felt faint because I hadn't eaten. I'm fine," I replied. "I admit it was strange to go through Amisihathor's belongings. But then, I've never had access to an ancient person's possessions before. I suppose archaeologists on digs are used to it. I wonder when I'll get to go on an excavation?"

"I might be able to pull a few strings," Kent said airily. "But I have an even more exciting prospect for you. How about supper with the family tomorrow night?"

Was this the equivalent of taking me home to meet his mother already? I was probably getting ahead of myself, but the thought was a pleasant one. "I'd love to," I said. "Shall I wear my gown and tiara?"

"Certainly, if you don't mind the rest of us laughing at you. Seriously, no call to get done up like a dog's dinner. A simple frock will be fine."

"Does that mean a basic black dress and no gloves?"

"I'm happy to see that along with German and French, you are familiar with the Queen's English. We'll have you speaking properly in no time. Shall I fetch you about sevenish?"

I agreed that sevenish would be fine. When I hung up the phone a few minutes later, I went into the kitchen for my long-delayed meal. I wasn't the least bit light-headed now. In fact, I seemed to have extra energy after my nap. What a curious dream that had been! It was more like watching a movie than experiencing the usual disjointed images. I knew that I would not be able to sleep until I had captured it on paper. Getting out my sketchpad, I began to bring the characters to life.

Chapter Ten

In spite of only four hours sleep, I sailed through the next day. Katy looked at me suspiciously as I sang while typing up a report. "What have you been up to, young lady? I've never seen you so cheerful this early in the morning."

"Just full of the joy of life. It's a beautiful world, Katy."

"Is it? I suppose so, as long as there's coffee in it. At least Briggs seems calm these days."

Thankfully, he was. He had a paper due for a meeting of the Archaeological Institute of America in New York, and the pressure of getting it done had made him quite irritable lately. He was a private man with a somewhat prickly personality, but in months of working together, we had developed a certain affinity. He was a brilliant scholar, and I had been very lucky to get a job with him. I earned money as well as credit towards my degree, and at the same time, I was gaining invaluable experience. Even on the professor's worst days, I had nothing to complain about.

"His paper is coming along nicely," I told Katy. "I even got a little reward for all my hard work." I took a plastic Starbucks card out of the drawer. "Here, I want you to have it. Splurge on some ventis."

"I couldn't take your hard-earned gift," Katy protested as she appropriated it gleefully. "I could not possibly go out at lunch for the largest size caramel macchiato! Would you like me to bring you anything while I am *not* doing that?"

"I'm fine. You drink to your heart's content."

"Thank you! I only accept because I know you now have a rich Brit wining and dining you, so you won't go without. Of course, you're keeping me updated on that front, aren't you?"

"Of course," I replied sweetly. But in reality, it was too personal to share just yet. I wanted to savor this wonderful feeling privately for a while.

Kent came to get me after work. He looked good enough to eat, dressed in a pair of brushed cotton pants and a crisp white shirt that settled nicely across his broad shoulders. "We're giving you a proper English meal," he teased as we drove over there. "Beans on toast, a packet of crisps, and digestive biscuits for afters."

"What, no Cock-a-Leekie soup?" I inquired.

"Wrong nationality, my dear girl. Have to get yourself a Scottish boyfriend if you want food like that. He could serve you haggis and oat cakes as well."

"Sounds tempting, but I'm satisfied with you for now," I smiled.

He leaned over to kiss me, but I pushed him away. "Watch the road, please! I'd hate to die before I could taste a digestive biscuit."

In fact, the dinner contained no such fare. It was an excellent soufflé that tasted like something you'd get in an elegant restaurant. There was also some delicious butternut squash soup, fresh steamed vegetables, and Sally Lunn bread. It was so far above my usual microwaved standard that I felt as though I'd wandered into Buckingham Palace by mistake. This was intensified by the presence of the cook who had prepared the whole repast. His name was Winston, but I had to bite my tongue to keep from referring to him as 'Jeeves.' He came out with each course, and hovered anxiously until someone said "Wonderful, Winston!" Then he would retire with a self-effacing nod. He saved the best for last, a raspberry trifle. He watched as I put the first spoonful to my lips. There was no need to feign enthusiasm.

"Winston," I said with a sigh, "this is absolutely heavenly!"

"Hear, hear!" Kent seconded. "You've outdone yourself. Cheers!"

The chef modestly accepted his due, murmuring, "Too kind," and "it was nothing." Dame Ursula looked after him fondly as he retreated.

"Such a talented man," she said. "And yet he's certain that every dish is going to be a disaster. He's been with us for many years, and we've never been able to dispel that notion."

"Does he come with you whenever you travel?" I asked, imagining such a luxury.

"It depends on where we go. He adores America," Ursula answered.

"He likes to find little diners and eat things like hotdogs and homefries," said Philip. "His favorite is called 'the garbage plate.'"

"Another local specialty," I supplied. "A hotdog, a hamburger, baked beans, bread, and macaroni salad, all covered in onions and hot sauce."

"Well," said Ursula tactfully, "I suppose our food might seem strange to other people."

"What's strange about bangers and mash, or bubble and squeak?" Kent winked at me. "Or toad in the hole?"

"Aside from the fact that they sound like rock bands, nothing, I'm sure!" I turned to Dame Ursula. "It's been such a lovely dinner," I said sincerely. "Thank you so much for asking me."

I really had had a wonderful time. In spite of their advantages, the family was not in the least pretentious. Our conversation was easy and wide-ranging, and they encouraged me to talk without being overt about it. Above all, they made me feel welcome.

"My dear, we are so glad to have you here. The pleasure is all ours."

Winston brought out a bottle of wine, completing my fantasy meal. We didn't actually adjourn to the drawing room, but the library was just as good. This, I thought, I could get used to.

After a while, Ursula announced, "I'm afraid Lily and I must talk shop for a few minutes. Could you boys excuse us?"

When Kent and Philip had departed, I handed over the portfolio I had brought with me. "I did these sketches last night," I said.

I had drawn the temple at Edfu, the revelries of the Feast, and the meeting of Amisihathor and Kamenwati. Ursula studied the pictures for a long time, then looked up with a smile of sheer delight. "These are wonderful, Lily! You've captured the scenes perfectly. Which festival is it?"

"The Feast of the Beautiful Reunion," I said.

"Ah, so that's where she met Kamenwati. He was a scribe in the temple of Horus. This is more than I dared hope for, to have you see so much, so soon! You are a very powerful medium, my dear. Soon, you will know how to help."

Exactly how she expected me to send two souls into the blessed afterlife, I didn't know. But at least she seemed happy. Perhaps a few more pictures would satisfy her that the couple was headed towards the Field of Reeds.

Ursula continued to pore over the sketches. "You have a wonderful eye for detail. Look at Amisihathor's earrings. So small, yet one can make out the interlacing wires inside the hoops and each little dangling bead. May I look over them until you leave?"

"Of course," I replied.

She patted my hand. "You're a special young woman, Lily. I'm glad that Kent is getting to know you. He's very fond of you already."

"I'm fond of him too," I said. "I think he's the nicest man I've ever met."

She beamed at me, not seeming to find the simple statement trite at all. "I'm sure he's waiting for you now with bated breath. You won't mind if we leave you two alone, I hope. I'm a little tired, and Philip has an errand to run. But I'll see you again before you go."

She took my drawings with her, and summoned Kent from somewhere in the huge house. He came back into the library with an expectant look.

"She loved them," I said, answering the unspoken question. "They made her happy."

Kent sat down, slipping his arm around my shoulders. "Good. But remember, love, anytime you want to stop, you only have to say so."

"I know. But it's fine." I lay my head on his chest. "I've really had a good time tonight. Dinner was fabulous."

"Winston is a marvel, isn't he? He came to live with us ten years ago, after his wife and daughter were killed in a car accident. At first, he drank a lot, but then Gram got him to attend

AA. I can't imagine the strength it took, but he's been sober for a long time now. I like to think he's found some peace."

My stereotype of the loyal family retainer was properly shattered. I reflected on how you could never really tell about other people's lives. "What a horrible thing to happen. Death is bad enough in any form, but something like that—" I shivered. "Poor Winston."

"Yes." We were quiet for a minute, and then Kent said softly, "My parents died together. They were in a small plane coming home from one of Dad's assignments. They got caught up in a storm, and lightning struck the plane. It went down in the mountains over Spain. To this day, I get edgy when I hear thunder. It's the sound of disaster."

I raised my head to gaze into his face, running my fingers down it tenderly. "I'm sorry," I said simply.

He took my hand, and kissed it. "I was six years old. It took me a long time to realize that I wasn't going to see them again. They were gone often, so I wasn't used to having them around. I thought they were just on another trip."

"It must have been hard for you," I said, my heart aching at the image of the little boy grown used to neglect.

"Yes, and no. I missed them. But I had my grandparents, and Philip. It was an exciting life for a kid. Very educational. I got to see a lot of things and meet unusual people. There was always someone coming to the house. One day, it was a chap with a collection of shrunken heads. He let Phil and me hold them. We were in our glory." Kent chuckled at my expression. "You might not understand the thrill, but we were boys! One Egyptologist brought a live cobra. Gramps wanted to try his hand at snake charming. Luckily, it stayed in its basket! Their bite can kill you within half an hour. I still remember the way the man described it, almost lovingly. He told us that a tiny bit of venom is incredibly toxic. Thousands of people die from them every year."

"You can see why the snake charmer was so popular in ancient Egypt," I remarked.

At this moment, Philip appeared in the doorway. "Sorry to intrude," he said, "but I left my address book in here, and I need it to make a call."

"That's fine," Kent said affably. He made no move to disengage himself from me, and I noted this with pleasure. "We were just discussing death by snake bite."

"And people say there's no romance in the world." Philip winked at me. "Ah well, mind you don't let him get started on those bloody Etruscans, or it will be death by boredom."

"Whereas manufacturing little sinks for people to spit into, and chairs to be tortured in is endlessly fascinating," his brother responded sarcastically.

This was obviously familiar banter between them. I raised my hand in a gesture of peace. "To each his own," I said. "But everyone knows that ancient Egypt is the most interesting topic there is."

"Gram will agree with you, so your numbers carry the day. I accept defeat," Kent declared graciously, "and place myself at your mercy." There was a gleam in his eye, and Philip coughed discreetly. "I'm off, then. Goodnight, Lily. I'm flying home tomorrow. Time and teeth wait for no man. It was a great pleasure to meet you."

I rose and shook his hand. "Likewise, Philip. Have a good trip."

I detected a hint of speculation in his smile. Was he wondering if he'd ever see me again? His departure brought home sharply the fact that Kent, too, must soon be going. I had shoved this realization into a corner in the excitement of getting to know him, but at this moment, it seemed to fill the whole room. Even as I returned to his embrace, I felt a knot in the pit of my stomach. What was I going to do when that time arrived?

Chapter Eleven

This thought was still haunting me the next day. I sat in front of my computer, staring at the screen listlessly. "What's wrong?" asked Katy. "Yesterday you were chirping like the first robin of spring, and today you look like the worm he ate."

"Where do you come up with these things?" I demanded. "'The worm he ate.' That's a nice image!"

"My writers' group thought so too," said Katy complacently. "I used it in my story, which, by the way, was greeted very favorably. I could go so far as to say that it enthralled them."

"Of course it did," I said. The story was about a character that strongly resembled Katy's boss, a scholar specializing in Arthurian Studies. The unfortunate fictional woman had many indignities inflicted upon her, depending on how Katy's dealings with her boss went. If Katy did not get her promised raise, the story lady was going to die at the reenactment of a joust. It was a colorful creation, and I always enjoyed reading the latest chapter. But today, I could not be distracted by it.

"Seriously, Lily. What's happened? You said dinner went very well."

"It did," I sighed. "That's the problem. It's all so great, I never want it to end."

"Well, it hasn't yet, has it?" asked Katy practically. "Shouldn't you postpone the pining until you're certain he's out of the picture?"

"That's easy for you to say," I replied irritably. Her cavalier attitude was wearing thin. "But it's not a game. I care about this man. I mean—" I was horrified to hear my voice crack a little bit —"I *really* care about him."

Katy looked distressed. "I didn't mean it that way! I—"

"Did you look at the sketches?" I asked brusquely. I had brought them in to show her that morning.

"I put them back on your desk," answered Katy in confusion. But before she could explain further, the red light on my telephone lit up. Dr. Briggs wanted to see me in his office.

"I've got to go," I said. "I'll talk to you later."

Briggs was ensconced behind his desk in a room where every available inch of space was taken up by books, papers, and replicas of Egyptian artifacts. Photographs of various digs and monuments covered the walls. There was a mummy case in one corner, and a scale model of the temple at Karnak perched atop a bookcase in another. The stone paperweight of a sphinx that I had given him for Christmas gazed solemnly at me as I sat down.

"Lily," he greeted me, with his customary brevity.

"Dr. Briggs," I replied, and waited. He was the stereotype of the absent-minded professor. It sometimes took him a minute to remember what he wanted to say. He was a handsome man with blond hair fading towards white, and blue eyes that always had a distracted look in them. It was only when he turned them on you that you could see the keen intelligence there.

"Lily," he said again. He reached into a drawer and, to my astonishment, pulled out my sketchpad. "This was on top of your desk. All your work?"

"Yes," I said in bewilderment.

"It's very good. Been thinking. Next book. Need illustrations. Interested?"

I could hardly believe my ears. "Are you serious, Dr. Briggs?"

"Yes. We work well together. Makes sense."

The University Press had published three of the professor's books on ancient Egypt, and they had all garnered critical and public acclaim. To be offered a chance to participate in that success was phenomenal. There was a ready-made market and a lot of exposure involved, not to mention a percentage of the profits. What a step up!

"I'm honored that you would consider me. This is such a surprise! What kind of time frame are we talking about?"

"Next six months or so. Started rough draft. I can give you a list and you can do some sample sketches for me. We'll go from there."

"Thank you, Dr Briggs. Thank you so much!"

I left his office in a kind of daze. I was bursting to share my news, but Katy was nowhere in sight. I went back to my desk and dialed Kent's cell phone. "Hello, love," he greeted me. "Are you at work?"

"Yes. And you won't believe what's happened! I just got an incredible offer; Dr. Briggs has asked me if I'd be interested in illustrating his next book!"

"Lily, that's wonderful! Of course I believe it. He'd be lucky to have you!"

"Can you come and celebrate with me tonight? This time, dinner will be *my* treat."

"I wish I could. But I've got a meeting with the director of the museum. Trade talk. Can we do it tomorrow instead?"

"Sure." I fought back a wave of disappointment. After all, Kent did have a life outside of me. "I'll keep the champagne on ice."

"I'm so pleased for you. You'll soon have a gallery of your own at this rate! You won't forget the little people, will you?"

"If you are referring to your six-foot-two-inch self, I assure you that I will not. Have a good time with your director. I'll see you tomorrow."

"Cheerio, and congratulations!"

Stupid museum, I thought childishly as I hung up. Well, perhaps I'd visit my mother tonight. I was overdue on that score. She'd be impressed, anyway.

My grumbling stomach reminded me that it was almost time for lunch. I'd brought a sandwich with me, but suddenly, that wasn't good enough. I decided to walk across campus and go to the inn that specialized in healthy food. Sometimes, I treated myself to their Moroccan Stew, a delicious blend of vegetables, cumin, and ginger. I still could not locate Katy, so I set off into the bright afternoon sunshine by myself. However, I was not destined to be alone for long. The first person I saw when I walked into the restaurant was Stephen.

"Lily!" He stood up from his table and held out his arms. I hugged him, then stepped back to return his smile. "I like the beard," I said.

"Thanks." He rubbed his hand over the neat goatee. "I had to do something. People were taking me for a first year student!"

I knew what he meant. Stephen had a fresh, youthful look about him, with close-cut sandy hair and big brown eyes. Even the stress of his profession had not added any lines to that smooth skin.

"The beard helps," I acknowledged. "Now you just need some thick, horn-rimmed glasses."

"A good idea in theory, but I don't want my patients thinking I might not be able to see!" He indicated the extra chair. "Can you sit down for awhile?"

"Sure," I said, and did so. "Have you ordered yet?"

"No. I've never been here before. It's nice and close to the hospital, though. When did it open?"

"About six months ago. The food is wonderful. Try the vegetable pita with tzaziki sauce. You'll like it."

"Okay. I'm game." He leaned back and smiled at me again. "It's so great to see you, Lily. You look happy. How's the job going?"

"Fine. It's been really interesting working with Dr. Briggs. And guess what he did today? He asked me if I'd consider illustrating his next book!"

Stephen whistled. "Hey, kid, you've hit the big time! I always knew you had the talent. Congratulations!"

"Thanks!" I said, feeling absurdly pleased with his approval. It had always been Stephen, the over-achiever, in the spotlight before. I realized that after a year of adjustments, I was coming into my own, and I liked it.

The waitress came and took our order, and Stephen and I chatted with no trace of awkwardness. I was surprised at how relaxed it was. It could have been falling into old patterns, but I preferred to think of it as a mark of maturity. We each felt comfortable enough with ourselves to *be* ourselves. Later, perhaps, we would talk about what had happened between us. But for now, I was relieved to simply be visiting with a friend.

We spent an hour at the restaurant, just catching up. He told me about his work, and listened attentively as I told him about mine. I mentioned meeting Dame Ursula and Kent, without going into detail, but Stephen knew me well. "So you're serious about him, Lily? I hope he's good enough for you." And that was all he said.

He insisted on paying for lunch when we were finished. "It's a celebration, isn't it? All the way around. And I still want to go out for drinks. Call me sometime, all right?"

I returned to the office in a much better mood than when I had left. It was elevated even higher when I saw a huge bouquet of flowers sitting on my desk. It was a stunning display of color in a milk-white vase, with a little teddy bear perched among the greenery. The card read 'Congratulations. Well done! Until tomorrow, love, Kent.'

I exclaimed out loud in delight, and Katy materialized by my side. "What did I tell you?" she asked. "No pining if you weren't sure he was going to leave. And it doesn't seem as if he intends to. Maybe he *really* cares about you, too."

I wrapped that thought around me like a soft blanket, and floated through the rest of the day.

Chapter Twelve

The next day seemed determined to bring me back down to Earth. I overslept by half an hour and awoke to find pouring rain, a soggy newspaper, and no milk in the house. I had forgotten this staple yesterday at the store, while remembering all of the exotic ingredients needed to make a special dish for Kent. At least I had my priorities straight, I thought wryly.

I rushed to get ready without the benefit of my powdered breakfast drink. The blouse I pulled from the closet had a stain on it. I cursed silently as I yanked another one from its hanger. It didn't match my pants as well, but it would have to do. I felt like a disheveled mess as I ran from the house to my car. After hitting every red light, I arrived at the University to find the last parking spot in the hinterlands of the vast lot. When I finally got inside, Dr. Briggs was waiting for me, looming in the doorway like Mt. Vesuvius about to erupt. "Lily! The AIA has moved up their deadline. I need all the reference checks for the paper finished!"

It always amazed me that Dr. Briggs, a man who made a living writing books and papers, could only muster up the minimum of words when speaking. Was he reluctant to toss them away on mere conversation? I was used to terse instructions from him, but today, it rather put me out. I resisted the urge to salute and say, "Yes, sir!" Instead, I went to my desk and got straight to work.

By ten-thirty I was so hungry that I had to stop and grab something to eat. Katy was getting a cup of coffee, and she looked at me sympathetically. "Old Briggs is on the warpath today, isn't he?" she asked.

"Blame the AIA." I took a sad-looking donut from the only remaining two in the box. "I don't know why they didn't clear their change of plans with me!"

"When you're famous, you can have someone to boss around," said Katy comfortingly. "I would have thought he'd be cozying up to you, now that you're practically related."

I shrugged. "All he said was, 'I understand you've met Dame Ursula. Fine woman.'"

"A big roadblock on Memory Lane? Well, no one ever called Briggs a chatterbox, did they? It's hard to imagine him being young and having a girlfriend. Yikes!" She picked up her cup hurriedly. "There he is, looking at us. Better get back to work, young lady!"

By the end of the day, I was only too happy to leave. The first thing I did when I got home was to check the answering machine. The blinking red light told me that I had a message, and I pushed the play button in anticipation.

"Lily, hi! Kent here. Can you ring me when you get home from work? I was wondering if I could come see you tonight. At the risk of sounding hopelessly gormless, I miss you. Thought perhaps you might like to go for a coffee or a walk or something. Sevenish? If you're not busy, ring me. Ta."

The tensions of the day fell away. I got a drink from the refrigerator, kicked off my shoes, and sprawled on the sofa. Cleocatra jumped up and settled herself on my lap. I stroked her thick fur with one hand and dialed the phone with the other.

"Hello, you've reached the voice mail of Kent Ashton. I'm sorry I'm not available to take your call at the moment. Please leave your name and number, and I'll get back to you as soon as possible. Thank you."

"Kent. It's me. I don't think you're gormless at all, because I have no idea what it means! I have yoga at six tonight, so if you want to come over about seven-thirty, that will be great! I'll see you then."

I hung up, leaned back, and closed my eyes. It felt good to relax. I thought of all the things that Kent and I had done in such a short time. I had been caught in a whirlwind, and I liked it. This romance might be unconventional, but it was exciting. This man was different from anyone I'd ever met before. Certainly different from the self-contained, practical Stephen. I remembered how proud I had been to introduce Kent to my friends on Saturday night. He had enjoyed the club, fitting in easily. He seemed to have a knack for that.

I allowed myself half an hour to lie there contentedly, then got up to feed Cleo. Thursday had been my yoga night for a while, and my classes started at six. I changed into my sweats and twisted my hair up in a ponytail. For a second, as I glanced in the mirror, I wondered what color a mix of gray and brown eyes would produce in a child. Then I laughed at myself and gathered my mat, a towel and some water into my duffel bag. Next, I would be writing 'Lily Ashton' on scraps of paper and designing wedding invitations!

I ate some fruit and cottage cheese and set off for the community center. One of my fellow practitioners was my friend Moira. Her red hair and alabaster skin were poster-girl Irish. "Hey, you!" she greeted me cheerfully. "How is your Brit?"

My Brit. I hugged the words to my heart. "He's great," I replied, unrolling my mat and sitting down on the floor beside her. We chatted until the instructor entered the room and began putting us through our paces. As I breathed and stretched and focused my mind, I felt it began to drift away. I was once again on the carousel with Kent, spinning around and around. Then in the garden, inhaling the scent of roses. Then in the car, pouring out my heart to him. And then...

The soft light of the moon is filling up the courtyard. It shows the low benches around the sacred sycamore tree where I am sitting. Beyond is the silvery shape of the temple, graceful and elegant. Far away, a wolf is howling, but I feel a sense of peace. Nothing can harm me here. Within these walls are warmth and safety and love.

I cannot sleep, for my heart is filled with thoughts of Kamenwati. It matters not that we have only just met. Who am I to question the wisdom of Hathor? For I know that she has sent him to me. I am content to leave my destiny in her hands. Somehow, she will see that we are together.

I am still wearing the garland of flowers that Kamenwati presented to me. Their perfume may have faded, but the memory of his fingers touching my skin will never lose its sweetness. I close my eyes, and see us standing in a garden, where grapes and roses and mandrakes grow, and of course, the lotus...

I was aware of someone saying my name.

"Lily! Yoo-hoo! Anybody home?"

I blinked as Moira waved her hand in front of my face. The rest of the class was on their feet, ready to practice the standing poses. As I rose also, Moira chuckled. "You *are* in love! Daydreaming away! Yoga isn't supposed to be so relaxing that you forget to move!"

I gave her a sheepish grin, and slowly balanced on one leg. I supposed you could call it daydreaming, but visions like that were the creative spark that made me want to paint. I knew that I would soon be sketching that courtyard. The images just rose up in my mind sometimes, so real that I could swear I was there. Just like the garden that had so impressed Ursula. What a coincidence *that* had turned out to be!

Returning home from class, I felt refreshed and invigorated. Was it the yoga, or was it because I knew I was seeing Kent? His car was already in the driveway, and my headlights illuminated him sitting on the front steps of my apartment. He waved as I pulled in, then came to open the door for me. He was holding a bunch of long-stemmed yellow roses, which he presented with a flourish. "Sweets for the sweet," he said grandly. "Of course, I use the term in the old-fashioned sense of 'flowers', not the modern one of 'candy'. However, if you would like some candy, I can get that as well."

"They're beautiful! Thank you so much!" I hugged him happily. It had been a long time since a man had given me flowers, let alone given them to me twice. "I couldn't possibly want anything more."

"I'm sorry to hear you say that," he replied, holding the embrace, "because I do, in fact, have more. But I don't want to overwhelm you."

It's too late for that, I thought. I took his hand. "Let me just enjoy these for a while, then. You haven't been waiting long, have you?"

"It seemed like forever." Then he diluted the romantic statement with a grin. "My word, I'm in top form tonight! Hugh Grant would be proud of me. I actually got here about five minutes ago. I wasn't sure how long it took to get your chi flowing smoothly."

"Chi is a Chinese concept," I informed him as I unlocked the front door. "Yoga is actually an Indian practice that frees up the life force. Similar idea, though."

Kent laughed. "We *are* academics, aren't we? We make a fine pair." He stepped uncertainly into the apartment. "Is that furry little monster anywhere about?"

On his brief, previous visit, Cleo had not exactly welcomed Kent. It was the first time I had ever seen her try to bite anyone. She appeared for a moment now, bristled at the sight of him, and stalked off.

"I'm sorry," I said as I turned on the lights. "I don't know what's wrong with her. Have a seat. Can I get you something to drink?"

"I'm fine, thanks." He stretched his lanky frame out on the sofa. "I feel so at home here, surrounded by books."

I did have shelf upon shelf stacked with volumes. I imagined how much more room there would be at Kent's house in Knightsbridge. "I hate to tell you this, but there isn't a single one about the Etruscans," I said, as if admitting a tragic flaw.

He gave a mock gasp. "Horrors! Well, we can remedy that. Don't despair. I'll loan you a couple of emergency paperbacks until we can get to a bookstore."

"You're an angel of mercy." I blew him a kiss as I went into the kitchen to fetch my one and only vase. I cut down the roses to fit in, and carried them back out to the coffee table. "Did you ever see anything so beautiful?" I asked as I admired them.

"Yes," said Kent.

I turned at the note in his voice, and the look on his face made my heart stand still. Silently, I sat down next to him, and slipped my arms around his waist as he pulled me close. It was like I was melting into him, his warmth and strength and sweetness, and a kiss had never felt so powerful and right. At last, I burrowed against him while he stroked me softly. Our idyll was rudely interrupted by a sudden hiss. Kent's lips moved against my hair. "It's the Cat of the Baskervilles," he murmured. "She's staring at us, and her eyes are glowing red."

I sat up reluctantly to look at Cleo. "Cleocatra," I said sternly, "what's your problem? Are you jealous?"

She meowed disdainfully, as if to say such an emotion was beneath her. Still, she stayed rooted to the spot, waving her tail back and forth.

I tried to reason with her. "I have fed you. I even gave you some milk. You have fresh water. What do you want?"

"For you to chuck me out," Kent supplied. "But that is not happening, cat. You'll just have to get used to me."

I liked the sound of that. "He's a very nice man, Cleo, really," I coaxed, holding out a hand to her. "Give him a chance."

My only response was the feline equivalent of a snort. "Fine, then, have it your own way." I snuggled back up to Kent, but after a minute, he disengaged himself gently. "It's no use," he said. "Her eyes are boring holes through me. Anyway, I told you I had something else to give you. I left it in the car. Won't be a tick."

When he was gone, Cleocatra jumped up on the couch and rubbed against me, purring. "Don't be so full of yourself," I told her as I stroked her fur. "He's coming right back. Why can't you behave? You never did this to Stephen. Be a good girl."

This, however, was not in the cards. As soon as Kent reappeared at the door, Cleo made a beeline for the bedroom, arching her back as she swept past him. Ignoring her, he set a box on the table. "One more kiss," he said, "and I'll show you what it is."

I was only too happy to oblige. But I was also curious. What could he have brought me? When I opened up the box, I couldn't believe what I saw.

Inside was a stunning piece of jewelry. Rows of beads, with a clasp of lotus blossoms held together by pearls. It was, in fact, a reproduction of Amisihathor's necklace.

I lifted it reverently. "Oh, Kent. It's absolutely amazing! Where on Earth did you find something so fabulous?"

He smiled. "A gentleman never tells. Let's just say I have my sources."

I fingered it in delight. "I never thought I'd have anything so beautiful. I won't say you shouldn't have, because I love it! Thank you, thank you, thank you!"

"Does that mean you like it?" he laughed, as I embraced him.

"I love it," I said softly, my lips against the skin of his throat. *And you*, I added silently. *My Kent.*

And the rest of the evening passed very pleasantly indeed.

Chapter Thirteen

Kent left at eleven. Normally, I would be winding down at this time, getting ready to sleep. But I was full of too much energy for that. I wanted to draw. I'd work on the scene that had come to me during my yoga class.

Before saying goodnight, Kent had fastened his gift around my neck. Now I went into the bathroom and gazed at my reflection. A thrill went through me. A different face seemed to shine out. It put me in mind of playing dress-up as a child. I knew it was myself that I saw, and yet it wasn't. I had a new power and a mysterious beauty that exhilarated me. I don't know how long I stood there, staring, but it was Cleocatra who brought me back to reality. She had come into the room and was yowling at the top of her voice.

"What's wrong?" I demanded. "You have been acting crazy tonight! Cleo! Stop that racket!" I reached down to her, but she backed away from me. I followed her to the hallway, wondering if there was something outside that had upset her. I checked the door and the windows; all was quiet. Probably a furry little denizen of the night was prowling about, and Cleo wanted to give chase. "Sorry," I told her. "Here, play with your mouse instead." But she ignored the stuffed toy I dropped at her feet, and stalked off to hide behind the couch.

"Be that way, then." I left her sulking and went to get my sketchbook. Settling into the big leather chair, I picked up my pencil and gazed at the blank sheet of paper. I always began this way, trying to make my mind a blank as well. When I felt calm and peaceful, scenes would begin to appear, developing slowly like a picture on film. Closing my eyes, I waited for the images to come.

I have seen the young scribe every day I have been at Edfu. Whenever my duties allow, I meet him. Sometimes, we sit in the temple courtyard, or walk about the grounds. He accompanies my sisters and I to the market, and ensures that we procure the best goods at the best price. He seems to know everyone in the town, and is always greeted with pleasure. I glow with pride when I see other women cast envious glances my way. Who would not want to be with a man as handsome and charming as Kamenwati?

Today, he has brought us a brace of birds that he himself killed. After leaving them with an adoring Tia, he and I stroll towards the river. "Where did you learn the skill of a hunter as well as the words of the gods?" I ask him, linking my arm through his.

"My father was a scribe to his Majesty Thutmosis, and was often at court," he replies. "My family lived on the estate of my uncle, Horemheb. His foreman took me to the marshes and taught me to hunt and fish. My uncle always said that a scribe could starve like any other man, but if you knew how to hunt, you would always be able to eat."

I do not think it likely that Kamenwati would ever starve. There is always work for scribes. It takes many years of studying at school, but one can rise to an exalted position with hard work, and the favor of the gods. I know that Kamenwati has ambitious plans, and I have no doubt that he will achieve them.

In our long talks, I have also told him about my home and my family. My father went into the West many years before, but left my mother with a comfortable income, so that we never wanted for anything. I had no brothers, but two uncles and numerous male cousins kept an eye on my older sister and I. At various times, any one or more of them might be staying with us. Then there is Kahotep, a priest at the temple. He is a great scholar who teaches reading and writing, and copies out important manuscripts. I have known him my whole life, and he has always been very kind. I know that my family expect us to marry, but Kahotep himself has never said anything of this to me. He loves me like a daughter, and I return his affection, but passion does not enter into it.

Kamenwati listens to everything I say with the utmost attention. I have never thought of myself as particularly interesting, but he certainly does. He discusses many things with me as an equal. He also praises my beauty. Men have commented on my looks before, but it has always washed over me. Hearing the words from Kamenwati gave them meaning for the first time.

Now, he is looking at me tenderly. "Never have I seen such perfect skin or eyes with such warmth in them. Ra has touched you, Amisihathor." His gaze moves up and down my body, and I shiver. "You are like a gazelle, with your long legs and slender, graceful form. Sometimes, I am afraid that if I touch you, you will bolt away into the trees and leave me desolate."

My voice catches in my throat. I can only whisper, "I will not leave you, Kamenwati." My eyes lock with his. "I will not run."

He bends his head down, and kisses me. His breath is as sweet as myrrh; it is like inhaling incense, intoxicating me. I press close against him, feeling as if his heart beats for both of us. I have no more control than a feather caught up by the wind. This is all I want out of life: to please the gods, and to be with Kamenwati.

I sat up suddenly. My neck was stiff and I had a cramp in one leg. I must have fallen asleep. My eyes went automatically to the clock on the desk. Midnight. An hour later than I last remembered. I checked the necklace, alarmed that I might have disturbed it, but not a bead was out of place. With a sigh of relief, I stretched and yawned. The dream was still vivid in my mind, and my fingers tingled with a familiar electric sensation. I had to get it down on paper. As I sketched, I considered how powerful suggestion could be. Here I was, conjuring up a whole life based on recent immersion in the world of Amisihathor. The images that became my paintings had often come with startling clarity, but not like the unfolding narrative of these dreams. Meeting Dame Ursula had done wonders for my creativity. And meeting her grandson had done wonders for me.

Chapter Fourteen

Ursula came over the next afternoon to look at all my work. I couldn't help but wonder what she thought of my modest apartment compared to her own establishments. Although she was not in the least bit haughty, she was a regal woman who was used to privilege. In spite of the warmth with which she treated me, did she really feel, deep down, that I was good enough for her grandson?

I had gone to an exorbitantly priced pastry store, and gotten cakes and scones to serve with tea. I had also borrowed china from my aunt. Mugs and mismatched plates would not do for Dame Ursula. Remembering her treatment of Kent, Cleo was banished to the bedroom. "And if I find any surprises in here," I told her sternly before shutting the door, "you will be one sorry cat!" She merely swished her tail in disdain.

Having duly imbibed and praised my tea, Ursula examined various pictures of mine carefully. Every once in a while, she would nod and smile in satisfaction. "These are simply extraordinary, Lily," she said at last. "There's no doubt in my mind that you are seeing things through the eyes of Amisihathor. I recognize several scenes from her daily life, and some of her belongings. These gaming pieces? And this cosmetic spoon? They're not part of the exhibition or the published catalog. Yet you have drawn them here. And this charming riverside tableau." She indicated the fruits of last night's labors. "It's just as we imagined the town of Edfu to be. Most impressive."

Strange thrills were going up and down my spine. It was puzzling, exciting, and disturbing, all at the same time. I could not explain what was happening. It was impossible to accept that an ancient Egyptian ghost was speaking to me. But I had to admit that my recent dreams were not ordinary ones either. I had always been possessed of a vivid artistic imagination. However, since I had touched Amisihathor's necklace, that creative spark had changed quality. Instead of occasional still photographs, I was now seeing a full color movie. My emotions were much more engaged. It was like a living story with real characters. And I realized that I was an integral part of it.

After Ursula eventually left, I did my yoga exercises, and then called my mother. I had spent a lot of time with Kent's family and he had not yet met mine. I wanted him to see the house I'd grown up in. My mother was a good cook who raised her own vegetables and herbs. She had loved preparing meals for Stephen. While I didn't expect the same amount of enthusiasm for Kent, I was sure she'd do herself proud.

I broached the subject after listening for five minutes about my Aunt Nancy's gallstones. "Mom," I said, "if you have a night free next week, I'd like to invite Kent over for dinner."

"I would *love* that!" she said enthusiastically. "What about Wednesday? I won't be playing bridge; Ken Bergstrom is having hernia surgery. I suppose we could ask the Heinleins as a substitute—if Maria can take her nose out of a book for long enough. Better say Tuesday, just in case. Is that all right?"

"I think so. I'll check to make sure and let you know. Do you want me to do the cooking?"

I knew perfectly well that my mother would not hear of such a thing, or miss the chance to get in a swipe at my culinary skills. I was right on both counts.

"No, no, I'd better do it. After all, I really enjoy it, and you – well, darling, no one is good at *everything*. I'll make my three-cheese lasagna and bake a loaf of Tuscan bread. Stephen loves Italian. And of course, I'll whip up a batch of oatmeal cookies! You just bring a bottle of nice red wine and leave the rest to me."

"Stephen?" I echoed in confusion. "Mom, I said—"

"It will be wonderful to see him again. I'm so glad you two have made it up. Or am I getting ahead of myself? I suppose it's too soon to tell, but you're making a nice start. There's no need to rush things. Nature will take its course. I'm certainly not going to be one of those awful mothers who try to tell their children what to do, but you know how I feel about Stephen. If ever there were two people who belonged together—"

"Mom!" I felt like I was trying to stick my finger in a dike. "I never mentioned Stephen! Stephen's got nothing to do with this! I want you to meet <u>Kent.</u> He's the one I'm dating, and he's the one I'm inviting. Kent!"

There was a moment of silence. Then my mother said flatly, "Oh. I see. Him. Well. Are you sure that's what you want to do?"

"Not anymore," I said in exasperation. "What have you got against him, except the fact that he's not Stephen?"

"You can hardly blame me for being partial," she said defensively. "I've known Stephen for years. I looked on him as a son. He's such a dear man, so responsible, so dedicated, a *doctor!*"

"Kent is dedicated and responsible too!" I retorted.

"He works in a museum," said my mother, in a tone that implied this was only one step up from male prostitution.

"Maybe the most famous museum in the world!" I said hotly. "He's an authority on the Etruscans!"

"Never heard of them." My mother was obviously not going to give an inch. "I just don't think he's good for you, Lily."

"How can you say that?" I asked, frustrated by her perversity. "Most mothers would drool at the very thought of a man like Kent. He's smart and kind and respectable enough for Queen Elizabeth! He's got a good job, is from a good family—what more do you want, for crying out loud?"

"An American would be nice," she replied, as unruffled as always by my agitation. "You just never know with foreigners, do you? You might go over to his country and not be able to get back. It happens, Lily. They've made movies about it."

"Mother," I said very slowly and loudly, "he is from England. <u>England!</u> We haven't had any problems with them since 1812. It's not exactly a political hotbed."

"It's a long way off," my mother replied stubbornly. "Different culture, different—customs." She gave the last word a sinister emphasis.

"Like what? Blood sacrifices at tea-time?" I was at the end of my patience now. "If you don't want to meet him, that's fine. Invite Stephen over and you two can have a great time. Maybe you can travel together to visit Kent and me when we're in London!"

But my mother, as always, had the last word. "You see what even *talking* about this man does to you? We'll speak later, after you've calmed down. Goodbye, Lily."

I was left with the immature urge to throw the phone across the room. I settled for stamping my foot and shouting into the air, "She drives me *crazy!*" Cleocatra looked at me without sympathy. *I deal with crazy all the time*, she seemed to say. The truth was, I was angry with myself as well. In spite of the fact that I knew my mother, and was always determined that I would not play her games, I still let her wind me up like a clock. I should accept that I was not going to change her and refuse to get upset. But I was a long way from mastering that skill. Instead, I had a large kahlua and milk and went to bed early with a book. I didn't care what my mother thought. Kent was perfect for me, and I was going to stick with him.

I returned home to Dendera with a very special gift. Kamenwati gave it to me on my last night in Edfu. It was a beautifully carved ivory scarab with outstretched wings.

"I had it made for you, my love," he said proudly. "I would not want you to forget me before we are together again! Wear it next to your heart and it shall protect you. I have inscribed it with my own hands." He laid a finger against the words etched onto the back. "'Sweetness to the flower of Hathor.' Ah, what sweetness you have brought to my life!"

My happiness was so intense, I could scarcely contain it. Kamenwati had decided to join me at the temple of Hathor and Horus in Dendera. I had trusted the goddess with my fate, and she had not disappointed me.

Until I met Kamenwati, my life had always been one of duty. I was happy to be in my honored position, to serve the goddess, to do as my family bid me and be content with their approval. But then that orderly life had been swept away like sand in a desert storm. For the first time, my feelings were deeply stirred. They no longer felt under control, which was frightening as well as intoxicating. Suddenly, my future was no longer laid out in a neat pattern.

I did not know what my uncle would say when I told him of Kamenwati. A scribe does not occupy the same exalted position as a priest of Horus. Nor does he have the same material means. Yet his is a respectable place, and his prospects of advancement are good. I did not believe Uncle would object too strenuously. As for Kahotep, he looks upon me more as a daughter than as a wife. He will have no trouble finding a suitable woman, one that can make him truly happy.

Or so I thought. But it was different when I sought him out at the temple to tell him my plans. What was it that I saw in his eyes? Sorrow? I felt a pang of remorse; Kahotep had sat me on his knee when I was a child, told me stories, taught me to read the words of the gods. It would hurt me to think he grieved at my choice. But his voice was steady when he spoke. "Is this what you truly desire, Amisi?" he asked me.

"With all my heart," I replied.

"Then your heart will not be denied. I will speak with this Kamenwati, and then with your uncle. May the blessings of Horus be with you."

I threw my arms around him in joyous affection. "Thank you, oh, thank you, dearest friend!" I cried.

And so it has been arranged. A contract has been drawn up. I am leaving my home to move in with Kamenwati and become his wife.

He is standing outside of his house, waiting for me. The last rays of the setting sun seem to make him glow. My heart leaps in my breast. "Kamenwati!" I cry, and run towards him.

He sweeps me up in a fierce embrace. His shoulders are so broad, his waist so slim, his skin so firm. Desire stirs in me, something I have never felt before. I know I have made the right decision.

Then his mouth comes down on mine. He carries me inside, kissing me all the while. I am trembling with excitement as he places me gently onto his bed. For a long moment, he looks into my eyes, and in his, I see my happiness, my future, my life. He removes my dress with a tug, then slips out of his tunic. How easily and naturally we come together, our limbs entwining perfectly, our rhythms like a song. Truly, Hathor has blessed us, for our bodies vibrate with joy. Afterwards, we go onto the rooftop and lie together, staring drowsily up at the stars. "There are the Imperishables," says my love softly, his eyes fixed on the horizon. "One day, we will go there together, and live among the gods."

It is good, so good, to be cradled in his arms, safe and satisfied, and know that we will never be parted. I turn my face away from the sky and press it into his shoulder. For now, my heaven is here.

Chapter Fifteen

The next afternoon, I had to take Cleo to the vet for her annual shots. It was hard to say which one of us dreaded this event more. She had been given tranquilizers to calm her down beforehand, but getting them inside her was a major challenge. She could smell one part pill to every ten parts of food I tried to hide it in. Somehow, she managed to consume a whole can of tuna fish and a piece of salmon without swallowing the least bit of medicine. When I attempted to put the pill in her mouth and massage her throat, she set up a wail that sounded as if I was skinning her. At last, I simply gave up, deciding not to exacerbate the ordeal any longer. I brought out her traveling cage and she stared at me fixedly. Her expression could not have said more clearly, "You've got to be kidding." I put her favorite stuffed mouse and a treat inside, and tried in vain to coax her.

"It's for your own good," I said desperately. "Do you want to get some horrible disease and die? Come on!"

Cleo was not moved by my plea, and I had to pick her up and deposit her behind the bars. She mewled mournfully through the entire drive, and my head was pounding by the time I reached the vet's. I reflected once again that the tranquilizers had been prescribed for the wrong party.

As I sat in the waiting room, I was amused to hear two women talking about the museum. "I don't like having that mummy in town!" said one. "It's bad luck. They're all cursed!"

The other nodded her head vigorously. "Remember what happened when King Tut went on tour? Accidents everywhere! There are some things that shouldn't be messed with. Leave them in their secret places, and let them lie in peace."

I was about to say that, actually, Egyptians did not want to lie forgotten. If no one visited their tombs and spoke their names aloud, it was a second death far worse than the first. But I didn't get the impression that they would welcome my input. If I argued with every person who labored under such misapprehensions, I would soon have no breath left.

"The lady who discovered this grave—an English lady, you know—the curse got her. It killed her daughter in a plane crash. And then her grandson's wife went crazy. She's locked up in Argentina or Africa or some such place. Doesn't really seem fair, her just marrying into the family—but I guess the mummy isn't too particular. This website says you can get cursed just by *looking* at the faces of the dead. I wouldn't go to that exhibit for all the tea in China."

I couldn't keep still any longer. "That is absolutely ridiculous!" I said indignantly. "I happen to know the grandsons and there is no wife, crazy or otherwise. There's no curse, either. It's all nonsense."

The women looked at me as if I had suddenly grown another head. The first one opened her mouth, but I was spared a confrontation by the appearance of the vet technician. "Archie is coming out of the anesthesia now, Mrs. Roth. You can come in and hold his paw if you'd like."

Mrs. Roth rose to do just that, apparently deciding it was beneath her dignity to speak to me. Her companion sniffed in my direction and then followed along behind the tech. Idiots, I thought crossly. Believing everything they read online. They probably subscribed to the <u>Weekly Enquirer</u> too. Slandering Kent's family when they didn't have the least idea what they were talking about made me angry.

When I was summoned for my turn inside the office, the doctor's assistant was waiting with gloves so thick, a lion couldn't penetrate them. She was experienced with Cleo by now. It took fifteen minutes to pry the stubborn cat out of the carrier. She had an amazing ability to stretch out all four legs and cling, limpet-like, to the bars. When she actually got onto the table, the noise she made was indescribable. Nails on a blackboard were melodious by comparison. With both the assistant and me holding her down, the doctor was able to give her the exam.

After it was over, Cleocatra purred all the way home, but I was far from happy. As silly as it was, I just had to call Kent and share my anger at the two women. He would laugh, and then I would feel better.

When I got inside the apartment, Cleo immediately ran under the bed. She would stay there until she deemed I had been sufficiently punished. As I was putting her toy into exile with her, the phone rang. I reached up from the floor and grabbed it. "Hello?"

"Lily. It's Kent."

"Kent!" I exclaimed. "I was just about to call you. You must be psychic!"

"Lily, listen." His serious tone sent a shiver through me. "Something has come up. There's been a family emergency."

"Ursula." My heart lurched. "Oh, Kent, is it Ursula?"

"No, Gram is fine. I'm sorry, but I can't really talk about it right now. I have to go back to England and take care of some things. When I've got it sorted out, I can explain, but I'm in a terrible rush at the moment. My plane's leaving in a few hours. I wanted to let you know, and I'll be in touch with you soon."

"Is there anything I can do?" I asked anxiously. "Do you need me?"

"It's very sweet of you, but I can handle it. I do wish I had a chance to say goodbye."

This time, my heart stopped. "Aren't you—aren't you coming back?" I stammered.

"Oh, yes, of course I am. I must be off now. I'll ring you as soon as I get to London. Right?"

"Right," I said mechanically.

"Bye then."

"Bye."

I felt as cold as if I'd stepped into ice water. Strange then, how the heat rose up in my throat and turned into a torrent of tears. I lay back on the floor and sobbed. Cleocatra came out of hiding in alarm. She rubbed against me, and I buried my face in her soft fur. "Oh, Cleo!" I wailed. "He's gone! He's gone already and he didn't even come to see me. What's happened? Why couldn't he tell me? What if I never see him again? Oh, Cleo!"

I blubbered on for some minutes, then slowly began to regain control. I sat up and blew my nose while Cleo batted at the box of tissues. "Go on, then," I said, giving her a few to shred. "You deserve it. What a day we've had, hey? But there's no sense in going to pieces, is there? Poor Kent has had some kind of family trouble, and here I am, feeling sorry for myself. Think of *him*. He said he would call me and I'm sure he will. Then I'll find out what I can do for him. And of course, he'll be back. He wouldn't lie. Hasn't everything been wonderful with him? It *has*. So I have no reason to be getting hysterical. Just stop it."

I received only a blizzard of flying tissue in reply, but I felt better. I went into the bathroom and washed my face. I didn't have to work today, and had planned on meeting Moira for lunch. That no longer appealed to me. I called her to cancel, and then the doorbell rang. Definitely not, I thought. The last thing I wanted right now was company. I ignored the sound until it stopped. But then a tap on the bedroom window nearly made me jump out of my skin. I spun around to see Stephen peering at me through the glass. Oh, great. "You scared me half to death!" I said loudly.

"Sorry, kid." He waved his hand in what I took to be an apologetic gesture. "But I saw your car so I figured you were home. Can I come in?"

I should have resented his easy familiarity, but instead, it was oddly comforting. I went around to the front to open the door. "What's wrong?" he asked immediately, upon sight of me. "You look terrible."

"Thanks a lot," I said, as he followed me inside. "I'm quite all right. I just got some upsetting news. There's a problem in Kent's family and he's had to go back to England."

"That's too bad. Is someone ill?"

I couldn't admit that I didn't know. "At least it's not Ursula," I hedged. "He'll call later with the details. It doesn't sound like anything he can't handle, but of course, it worries me."

"Naturally. And speaking of worry…well, I saw your Mom last night."

I groaned. "Stephen, please tell me that she didn't send you over here to check on me. What kind of nonsense has she been bothering you with?"

We were sitting on the couch by now, and Cleocatra had come out to rub against Stephen's leg. "Hello, Cleo," he greeted her. "How have you been? You're more beautiful than ever. Yes you are," he said, as he stroked her black fur.

Cleo purred and blinked, for all the world as if she were batting her lashes. She couldn't have looked less like the spitting she-beast of the morning.

"Stephen?" I prompted. "Mom?"

"She called to invite me over to dinner. Naturally, I accepted. I missed her cooking. I get tired of grabbing something out all the time, and hospital food is not my favorite. She made lasagna, and it was *great*."

"Never mind the menu," I said impatiently. "What did she tell you about *me*?"

"Well, basically, she just hinted that you and I should not have drifted apart." He paused. Drifted apart? I thought. Is that how he had reframed not having any time for me?

Stephen continued, "She thinks we're meant to be together, and practically asked me if I was going to save you from this dangerous foreigner."

"She's never even met him!" I exclaimed. "Honestly, that woman! I don't know what her problem is. Except for the fact that she dotes on you."

"Can I help it if I'm irresistible?" he quipped, but seeing my expression, he quickly stifled his grin. "I'm sorry if it embarrasses you. But your mother is a lot smarter than I was; I shouldn't have let you slip away. I know it's water under the bridge now. I just wonder if Kent is right for you."

Stephen's admission might have hit me like a thunderbolt if I hadn't already been struck by lightning. As it was, I skipped right over his declaration and jumped in to defend Kent. "He is an absolutely wonderful man," I declared. "And what if he weren't, anyway? I would figure it out. I can take care of myself."

"Sure you can," Stephen agreed equably. "That doesn't mean that no one's going to worry."

"Well, there's nothing to worry *about*," I said firmly. "I'm dating a great guy, I'm having fun, and I'm happy."

"Oh, *that's* why your eyes are all red," Stephen replied mildly.

I glared at him. "Kent is having trouble right now. Of course that makes me sad!"

"But he has to fly three thousand miles away to settle it. Because that's where he lives."

"Stephen." I kept my rising temper with an effort. "Can I politely say that this is none of your business? If you don't want to talk about something else, it would be best for you to leave. The day's been hard enough already."

"Tell you what, then." He surprised me by getting up and holding out his hand. "Let's go to Reed's and have banana splits. My treat. Remember what you used to say? 'There's nothing a banana split won't make better.' Don't suppose you've changed your mind?"

I couldn't help smiling. "It's a good philosophy, and I've stuck with it."

"All right. That's what the doctor orders. And we'll bring back a dish for Cleo."

So we went, and it did make me feel better. But I fell asleep that night with the cell phone beside my pillow, and no word from Kent.

Kamenwati and I have been very happy. I am proud of his success. He has risen in the ranks at the temple, as I knew he would. He is away from me a great deal, but that is necessary. How else will he advance? He is pleased with our new house, its painted walls and fine wooden furniture; but both of us enjoy our garden the most. When he is home, we sit under the shade from the trees and delight in the beauty and sweet scents of the flowers. It was on one such day that Kamenwati presented me with the finest gift of my life.

"It is time you had such adornment as befits you, my wife," he said. *"See what I have ordered the jeweler to make."*

My eyes were dazzled. The necklace was filled with rows of beads of many colors. Two large lotus blossoms of deep blue were fastened on the ends, and also a string of pearls for holding it about my neck. I turned it over in my hands rapturously, as Kamenwati continued.

"The turquoise is blue like the cornflowers here in our garden; the carnelian is red as the poppies; and the green is the color of the papyrus. Surely that and the lotus will bring us fertility and we will celebrate new birth."

It has not pleased the gods to send us any children yet. I pray and make offerings to Hathor and Tausret, and trust that one day, our house will be filled with sons and daughters to be the delight of our old age, and keep us in the afterlife.

I have shared all of my goods with Kamenwati, and we are quite comfortable. Work has begun on our tomb and on a copy of the book of Coming Forth by Day, so we shall be well prepared for our journey through the afterworld. Kamenwati works so hard, it is not surprising that he gets tired sometimes, and loses his temper. He is always sorry afterwards. It was the same for my mother and my father. No two people live together in perfection.

I am waiting for Kamenwati to come home this evening. A dinner of antelope and honeyed figs has been prepared. Sitting on our portico, I see him approach and rise to meet him. But something is wrong. He is in a state of great agitation. I pour him some wine, but he does not drink it. Neither will he sit down. Instead, he is pacing like a wild animal.

"It is a disgrace," he mutters, "an insult! Why do they deny me what is mine? I am skilled; I deserve to do more than write letters and draw up contracts! I will not be treated this way!"

"Calm yourself, my love." I try to take his arm, but he pulls away from me. "It's that old man!" he fumes. "He's never forgiven us for being married. Now he delights in keeping me down. I will never advance while he is in charge!"

I am shocked. "You cannot mean Kahotep? He has been so kind to us! Tell me what has happened. What troubles you so?"

"Kind!" Kamenwati repeats the word as if it is a curse. I have never seen him so angry. "Yes, that is what he would have us think! He has given me no more than is my due, yet I am expected to be grateful like a well-fed dog! And just like a dog, I am supposed to know my place and never beg for more! 'You are

too young to work on the sacred books,' he tells me. 'When you have been among us longer, we shall see.' Pah! Younger men than I have been elevated. It is jealousy, simple and sure. Kahotep fears that I am a threat to him, and he wants power only for himself!"

While not believing this to be true, I nevertheless try to soothe my husband. "Your cleverness has not gone unnoticed. You have been promoted once, and you will be again. It will only take time—"

Kamenwati's eyes blaze. "You are a fool, Amisihathor! Can't you see what I have been telling you? Kahotep has me under his heel, and I will stay there as long as he lives!"

Tears spring to my eyes. I know that he is not himself, but it hurts to bear his anger. As if suddenly understanding this, Kamenwati's face softens. He seems to collect himself with an effort. "Sister, forgive my harsh words. This has overmastered me. I had such hopes, not for myself alone, but for the two of us. If I advanced at the temple, you would have all the things you deserve. A bigger house, more servants, many more pieces of jewelry. Everything you would have had if you had married Kahotep."

In a rush of emotion, I fling my arms about him. "If that was what I wanted, I would have married him," I say. "But the happiness of my heart was far more important. I need nothing besides your love, Kamenwati."

Even as he holds me close, I hear his deep sigh. "I would that were true, my beautiful one. But life is not so kind. It is my duty to see that you are cared for, always. And I will do it."

Chapter Sixteen

"Are you telling me that you went on a *date* with Stephen?" Katy asked incredulously.

"No." We were eating lunch in the University cafeteria, and I stabbed at a wayward shrimp with my fork. "I'm telling you that we had ice cream together. He was trying to cheer me up."

"Uh-*huh*. And this is after he admits that he still loves you."

"He didn't exactly say that."

"Of course he did, you ninny! He comes back and sees that you have an exotic new boyfriend, and it makes him jealous. So he starts messing with your head. Not at all nice when you're vulnerable."

I sighed, pushing my salad away. I didn't have much of an appetite. I still hadn't heard from Kent, and anxiety was gnawing at me. I didn't have the energy to argue with Katy.

"Life was so much easier when all the men in my world had been dead for at least three thousand years," I said morosely.

"Well, if you want one that is not actually mummified, I suggest that you start fresh. Many a happy relationship has formed from a personal ad. Here, I'll write one for you." Katy got a pen from her purse and began scribbling on a napkin. "Beautiful woman, twenty-six years of age. Five feet two inches tall. Petite with dark hair, dark eyes and dazzling smile. Smart, sweet, great sense of humor. Seeks a male soul mate. Sanity preferred, but not essential. No physicians or Englishmen need apply."

I chuckled in spite of myself. "Thanks, but I'll stick with the ancient variety of male. I've sketched a few for Dr. Briggs. I'm bringing in my portfolio tomorrow. I hope he likes what I've done."

"I'm sure he will. You're a great artist, Lily. You can illustrate the covers of all my best sellers. We'll be as famous as the Captain and Tenille."

I knew she meant Lewis Carroll and John Tenniel of <u>Alice in Wonderland</u> fame. I made a face at her bad wordplay, but she just laughed. "Money will keep us together! We'll be rich enough to pay for assisted living in our old age, and we won't need men at all!"

It wasn't that simple, though. As I sat in my apartment that evening, I tried to distract myself with a rented movie, but everything in it reminded me of Kent. What was he going through? When would he be coming back? I debated with myself for a while, but the urge to know something, anything, was too strong. Finally, I telephoned Dame Ursula.

Winston answered the call, and said that her ladyship was 'occupied.' Could I wait? I did, biting my nails nervously until her cultured tones came on the line. "Lily, my dear." There was something else in the voice. Fear? "I'm glad to get the chance to speak with you. I'm preparing to return to London."

"Kent told me there had been a family emergency. He didn't have time to explain, but I've been so worried. Is there anything I can do?"

She sighed, and was silent for a moment. "Just be there for him, Lily. He needs you. I'm afraid that I can't say more than that. I know it's difficult, and I'm sorry. But there are things that you are not yet aware of, and when you know everything, I hope that you will understand, and forgive."

My stomach had tied itself up in knots. What was she saying? "Ursula, I *don't* understand," I said plaintively. "Please, can't you tell me what's wrong? Is Kent all right?"

Instead of answering my question, she surprised me with one of her own. "Do you love my grandson, Lily?"

I was taken off guard and overwrought, and so I blurted out the truth. "Yes," I said.

"Good. I knew I was not mistaken in you. Kent will be back, and you will have all your answers then. Thank you, my dear. I really must go now. We will talk again. Goodbye."

I sat holding the phone for a minute after she had hung up. Only when the mechanical voice announced that the line was temporarily disconnected did I put the receiver down. Disconnected. That was just how I felt. Nothing made sense anymore. I had been like a giddy child, spinning around and around until the fun gave way to dizziness and nausea, and all sense of direction was gone. What kind of trouble was Kent facing? What dark secret would he reveal to me upon his return? If, in fact, he *did* return. It was getting harder to convince myself that he would. How long could it be for, anyway? His job and his life were in England. It was possible not to think of that when he was beside me, but impossible *not* to think of it when he wasn't.

I lay awake for a long time that night, trying to force my mind into more positive channels. Remember, I told myself, you are going to illustrate a book! It will be the most challenging and rewarding work you've ever done. A career in art is no longer just a dream. And you did it all yourself. My thoughts drifted to childhood memories of my Dad hanging up each picture I drew, and showing them off to everyone who entered the house. How proud he would be of me now. It was this thought that finally comforted me enough to sleep. But it was not to be an easy slumber.

"Are you all right, mistress?" asks Tia, looking at my face in concern.

I say simply and untruthfully, "Yes. It is so close today, that is all."

The air is indeed oppressive. It almost hurts to breathe it in. My sleep was broken by nightmares in which I was being sealed in my own tomb. I tried to call out, but no one could hear me. I awoke gasping for breath, and damp with perspiration. The terror of it continues to take its toll this morning. I am restless and uneasy, unable to settle down to anything. After pricking my finger several times, I abandon my needlework and seek solace in the garden. Perhaps among the trees and flowers, I can rid myself of the nerves that assail me. I am drawn to the cool waters and the fish swimming therein. When I was a child and visiting the house of Kahotep, the pool was my favorite spot. I loved the blue tiles that lined it, the lotus blossoms floating on the surface, the different creatures that lived there. Sometimes, I would see turtles climbing onto the rocks around the trees, and I was filled with delight. Our own pool is much less grand, but it is dear to my heart as well. It affords me great peace.

"Leave me for awhile," I tell Tia. "I wish to sit in silence."

But even this does not calm me. I need to go to the temple and seek out the proper priest. He will be able to interpret my dreams, and give me a remedy. Rising with a new determination, I put on my shawl and leave my house to go out into the street. Tia runs along behind me like an anxious shadow. "Mistress," she protests, "I do not think that it is wise to journey forth today. Recall that the master said you were to rest."

"I need to see the wise man," I reply, "in order to feel better. There is no need for you to come, Tia. I will be quite all right."

She is not happy, but says no more. I walk through the town, exchanging greetings with neighbors absently, only taking genuine notice of little Meretsankh, the beer-maker's daughter. She is pulling a carved wooden horse on a rope, and giggles in delight when I stop to pat its head. My heart swells with tenderness each time I see this beautiful child. I have not yet fulfilled my duty of bringing forth one of my own. Perhaps I will ask the amulet man for another charm to help me. Musing on these matters, I draw near the temple walls. The sight of the god's house never fails to move me. It is a splendid, sacred place, full of mystery and awe, yet also of strength and comfort.

For many years, it was more of a home to me than the house I lived in. When my father passed on and my mother had no time for me, I was always welcome here. Kahotep was kind to me, and I learned to serve the goddess, giving my life purpose. I will stop and visit with Kahotep today, I decide, after I have seen the priest. My husband is absent, at the great estate of a lord drawing up household contracts. He has promised to be home for the evening meal. He has been distant of late, worn down by his hard work. He is so determined to succeed and provide his family with every material comfort. When our children come, he says, they will want for nothing.

I am thinking of him as I walk past the mighty pillars, so that for a moment, I wonder if I have imagined his voice. It seems to be coming from beyond the doorway into the next hall. I stop in my tracks, but of course, it cannot be him. I am about to go on when I hear it again. This time, there is no mistaking the voice of

Kamenwati. It is faint, and I cannot make out the words, but I know that it is he. I follow the sound into the shadows. He has returned from the lord's house early, and should indeed be home this evening. Perhaps we can walk back together. He is speaking with someone now, though, and they are moving off ahead of me. I tread softly behind. I wish to see him, but I do not want to interrupt any temple business. I will wait nearby until he is done.

Then, suddenly, I catch a glimpse of him as he crosses in front of a torch on the wall. And I see his companion also. I am startled to recognize Kepi, a young priestess who has recently come among us. And I am more than startled by the way they are looking at each other. I am sickened. For in that glance is naked desire, which hits me like a thunderbolt of Ra. I pull back instinctively behind a pillar, just as they check to make sure no one observes them. Their hands touch briefly, and then they steal even further into the temple. Carefully, hardly knowing what I am doing, I creep after them.

They find an alcove and I hide behind a statue of his Majesty King Amenhotep. My heart is in my throat and I want desperately to shut my eyes, but I also must see what happens. Kamenwati pulls Kepi to him and kisses her roughly, sliding his hand inside of her tunic. I have to bite my tongue to keep from crying out, but the pain is nothing compared to the crushing weight on my soul. They are attacking each other like crocodiles in the Nile. I almost crumple where I stand, but then Kepi breaks away. "When, when will we be free?" she whispers fiercely. "You have promised me, Kamenwati! I would live by your side and share all with you. Yet you tarry, while our sons wait to be born! I cannot endure it!"

"My love," he says soothingly, "I have told you. I cannot set aside Amisihathor while the old priest lives. He would cause me to lose everything."

There is fire in Kepi's eyes. It freezes my very blood. "Then he should not live!" she hisses. "What right does he have to stand in our way? His day is past. You should be in his place. How often have you said so yourself? Are you no longer resolved to be rid of him? Do you wish to be a junior clerk with a barren wife all of your life?"

"I know what I must do, mistress," says Kamenwati harshly. "Do not doubt me! I have my plans. Kahotep will be gone by the time of the harvest. After that, nothing will stop us."

"Nothing," she repeats, flinging herself against him.

They are far too busy to be distracted. I back up as quietly as I can, which is easy, since I have no substance. I am no longer flesh and blood, but a ghost. And like a ghost, I flit quickly away.

Chapter Seventeen

When I awoke the next morning, I could not shake off the effect of my nightmare. I kept telling myself that it was my own emotional turmoil that was causing these vivid dreams. I was imagining feelings from Amisihathor that paralleled what I was experiencing. But of course, I had no idea what had really happened to her. It was all ridiculous. As ridiculous as supposing that Kent had rushed off to England because of another woman. What next, Lily? I asked myself sternly. Going to see the wise man for an amulet? You had far better keep your mind on your portfolio.

I did try to sketch, but it wasn't easy to concentrate. I gave up and went into the kitchen to grab a muffin. I had just bitten into it when the telephone rang. My heart leapt, and I ran to answer it. A familiar voice greeted me, but not the one I was hoping to hear.

"Lily, is that you?"

I repressed a sigh. "Hi, Mom."

"I've got your insurance bill. It came in the mail yesterday. You would think after six months, they'd have your new address on record."

"I know," I agreed. "I've called them often enough. Well, I'll stop by after work and pick it up."

"All right. I'll make you something to eat. Do you suppose Stephen—"

"Sorry, Mom, I have to go. The doorbell's ringing. Bye!"

Ay-yi-freakin'-ay. The woman was never going to give up. As if that wasn't irritating enough, I had forgotten that the bi-yearly life insurance bill was due. I'd have to readjust my budget to pay it. Come to think of it, I had never removed Stephen as my beneficiary. I'd have to call the company yet again. But I couldn't bother with it now. The extra hour I'd allotted for drawing had elapsed with absolutely no progress. It was time to go to work.

The day was quiet. Dr. Briggs was not in the office, and I read some articles about the origin of certain ancient Egyptian glass. It was used in some of the most exquisite jewelry, including the regalia of King Tut, and scientists were positing that perhaps it had come from a meteorite. It was a fascinating hypothesis, and much more engrossing than the scholarly footnotes I had to spend the afternoon working on. I left an hour early and drove out to the leafy green suburb where my mother lived, and I had grown up. As I pulled up to the split-level stucco, I felt the same slight sense of disturbance that I did every time I visited my old home. There were still traces of my father—the trees he'd planted in the yard, the antique coat-rack he'd inherited from his grandmother—but for the most part, his spirit was gone. The house reflected my mother's tastes, almost as if he had never lived there. She said that constant reminders were too painful, and his personal possessions had long been packed away. His study became a guest bedroom, his golf clubs and tools went to friends of the family. Only one picture remained on display. It was a large studio portrait of the three of us, made the year before he died. It now sat on the mantle with my graduation photo on one side, and a snapshot of Stephen and me on the other.

It was only with maturity that I understood my mother's way of grieving. At the time, I needed the physical trappings that made me feel my father was not truly gone. I wanted everything exactly the way it had been. I kept a paperweight I had made him for his birthday on the nightstand by my bed. I still had it now, sitting on my own desk. It was my most prized possession. Nothing in my old home brought him back clearly anymore, but when I looked at that paperweight, his image rose up like a bright light illuminating my mind. He had acted as thrilled as if I'd given him a treasure chest of gold. I had encased a drawing of him in round glass, and he told me that one day, after I was famous, they would want it for a museum; but he would never give it up. "Not for a million dollars, Princess," he promised. And not for a million dollars would I give up that memory of him.

My mother was in the kitchen. "Hello, dear," she greeted me. "I made a nice fruit salad, why don't you take it out of the refrigerator and I'll heat up the casserole."

I set the table while she bustled about getting our dinner. We talked in a desultory way about work, her bad back, and—surprise, surprise—Stephen.

"He's absolutely thrilled by your new book," she told me. "Wouldn't it be nice to have a husband who supported your career so strongly?"

"Mom," I said, "Stephen is happy for me because he's my friend. My *friend*. That's all there is to it."

"Of course," she agreed. But it was the same way she had answered me when I used to tell her that fairies lived in the back yard. It was obvious that she did not believe it.

One subject I didn't mention was Kent. Since she'd never shown any interest in him, I was not about to tell her that he was gone. She would put the worst possible interpretation on it. I was perilously close to doing that myself. By the end of the meal, I was feeling tired and despondent and I couldn't finish my dessert. My mother regarded me critically. "Wildberry pie is one of your favorites, and you've hardly touched it," she observed. "You don't look well, Lily. There are circles under your eyes. Haven't you been sleeping lately?"

The strange dreams haunting my nights were the very last thing I wanted to discuss. "I'm all right," I answered. "There's just been a lot going on."

"You've been acting strangely ever since you met this Kent character. Now, don't get angry, dear. I only want what's best for you, and I can't help worrying. Talk to Stephen and make sure there's nothing wrong. It's very useful to have a doctor as a –friend."

"Fine," I said, just to pacify her. I wanted to get home and go to bed. Perhaps Kent would call. But it was another half an hour before I could make a graceful exit. My mother insisted on packing up leftovers for me, throwing in enough groceries to last for a week. "Here you are," she said, handing me a heavy shopping bag. "Is there anything else you need? Do you have the money to pay that insurance bill? I'd be glad to help out."

"Thanks, Mom," I replied, "but it's okay. I can manage. I really appreciate the offer, though." I kissed her goodbye and made my way to the door. My mother opened it and slowly walked me out to the car. As I was about to get in, she exclaimed, "Oh, wait! I forgot your pie. I cut you a slice and left it in the refrigerator. Dear me, I'm getting so absent-minded. I hope it doesn't mean anything serious. I would hate to think I'm getting too old to be left on my own." She gave a tragic sigh. "I'll just go back and get it."

Nice try, Mom, I thought. The gratitude her generosity had produced in me dissipated, and I said, a little impatiently, "You seem as sharp as a tack to me. You'll be taking care of yourself for a long time to come, I'm sure. No, don't make another trip. I'll get the pie."

"In the white container, on the top shelf!" she called after me as I went back into the house.

Opening the refrigerator, I bypassed the lone slice and took instead the remains of the whole pie. That was the least I deserved. While I was hiding it in a plastic bag, the telephone rang. It was the notorious book-addicted Mrs. Heinlein. "Mom's outside," I told her. "If you can hold on, I'll get her."

I was both amused and exasperated when my mother forgot her decrepitude in her haste to talk to her friend. She came up the walk at a pace belying any infirmity. Probably couldn't wait to discuss the new man in her daughter's life.

And what of that man? I wondered as I drove back to my apartment. It was a beautiful evening, warm and clear. I passed hedges by the roadside teeming with fireflies, and my heart swelled with longing. "I'll see him again soon. I know I will," I said aloud.

But there was no word from Kent that night, and by the time I fell asleep with Cleocatra curled at my feet, despair was creeping into my heart.

I have found the dwarf, and I hurry after him. He is a trusted advisor who will be able to help me. "Master Sennemut!" I call.

The little man turns around to look at me. "Yes, mistress?" he asks politely.

"Can you tell me where Kahotep is? I must speak with him right away." *My voice is trembling, and I know I look in a dreadful state. Indeed, I have the feeling that I am on the verge of breaking, like a creation of the glassmaker's as it comes off the pipe. One breath too many, one lick of heat too much—or one thought of Kamenwati's lips on Kepi's—and I will shatter into so many pieces that I can never be made whole again.*

Sennemut does not question me, however. He simply says, "Follow me, mistress." *I stumble along behind him; my eyes are burning with unshed tears, my breath rasping in my throat. We make our way to the back of the temple where the House of Life is located. Only one thought keeps me going—to find Kahotep.*

And at last, I do. He is seated reading a papyrus scroll. His look of astonishment gives way to one of worry. As he comes forward to greet me, Sennemut discreetly withdraws. I am alone with my old friend, who asks me in concern, "Amisi, what has happened?"

The pain is raging in my chest, and suddenly, I cannot keep it in any longer. A great sob rises from within me, tearing at my throat. I crumple as the tears come, and Kahotep catches me. "Oh, my dear," *he says softly, over and over again, as the grief pours out. He rocks me back and forth like a child. I cannot speak, cannot think, for misery. After a time, I dimly perceive that I am gulping for air. Kahotep releases me from his arms and presses a cloth into my hands.* "I will get you a cooling drink that will calm you. Perhaps it may offer some ease."

I wipe at my face as he leaves me. I know I must tell him my story, but the words it will take are as dangerous and deadly as snakes. When Kahotep returns, I accept the cup he gives me. "Thank you. You are very good to me; you have always been very good. I cannot allow you to be hurt. That is why I must warn you, even though"—*my voice does not want to leave my throat, but I force it to go on –* "even though it is like cutting out my own heart to tell you. O, Kahotep, you are in danger! You must see that my—that Kamenwati is banished from Dendera!"

His look is sharp. "What are you telling me, child? What has the scribe done?"

Susan Mcleod

Slowly and painfully, I relate my story. I see shock, outrage, sympathy, and anger in Kahotep's face. He does not speak for a while when I am finished, just pats my shoulder and stares into the distance. At last, his eyes meet mine again. "Amisihathor," he says firmly, "you must leave your home immediately. You are not safe there. Bring any valuables that you possess here to the temple. We will explain that you are staying to have your dreams interpreted." I had forgotten in the chaos that this was the original reason for my visit today. "Go now, before the scribe can know of it. When you return, we will talk further. Sennenmut will escort you. You have been very brave, but you will need to keep up your courage. Much depends on it. Do you understand?"

I nod tearfully. There is a mute appeal in my eyes, which Kahotep recognizes. "I promise, I will not take any action before we speak again. And whatever happens, I will care for you. You have accomplished maat, and are a thousand thousand times more worthy than the evil scribe. He does not deserve to have Ra shine upon him. Go with Hathor and Horus, little one. I will see you soon."

He summons the dwarf to accompany me. I begin the journey back to the house like one in a bad dream. Can my life really have changed so completely since I walked on this road such a short time ago? It seems impossible. And yet I am returning a different woman. The former Amisihathor has died, and I do not know what kind of life this new one faces.

Chapter Eighteen

Luckily, work kept me occupied the next day. I was so busy that it was time to go home before I realized it. "Come on, I'll take you out for a drink," Katy offered as she shut down her computer. "Take pity on a girl who's all alone tonight."

I knew that it was me she was taking pity on. She must think that Kent was gone for good. Why, oh why hadn't he called me? I fought not to get sucked into that black hole again.

"Thanks, Katy, but I'm going to stay behind until I can talk to Dr. Briggs. I haven't seen him since we had coffee this morning, and all he could focus on then was his paper. I really want to show him the sketches I've done."

"Okay," she shrugged. "Give me a call later, and tell me what he thinks."

"Will do," I promised.

I was regretting my decision half an hour later when the building was empty and there was still no sign of Briggs. I knew he wouldn't leave without locking up his office, and the door was still ajar. At last, I went in to see if he had left any indication of his whereabouts. He must have been called away in a hurry, because the top drawer of his desk was sticking out. I glanced into it idly, and for a moment, my heart seemed to stop beating. It took my brain a second to catch up to my instinctive reaction. For lying there was an ivory scarab with outstretched wings. Even before I picked it up to look, I knew what it was going to say. Turning it over, I read the words, 'Sweetness to the flower of Hathor.'

"What are you doing?"

A voice recalled me to the here and now. It was abrupt and angry. Dr. Briggs had entered the room and he moved quickly to take the scarab away from me. "That's a very valuable piece, Lily," he said roughly. "I never expected to find you going through my desk and bothering things."

"I'm sorry," I said distractedly. "I didn't mean to—the drawer was open, and it caught my eye. It was so beautiful—I just didn't think. I only wanted to look at it."

"Well, you shouldn't have." He eyed me suspiciously. "It's late. Why are you here at all?"

I pointed to the papers I had put down on his desk. "I brought some of my sketches to show you. I worked on them all night, and I was anxious to see what you thought. You weren't in earlier, so when I saw that your office was still open, I waited. I thought you might have left a note or something. I'm really very sorry," I repeated lamely. "I didn't intend to pry. I'll go now."

I picked up the drawings hastily, preparing to flee. But Briggs reached the door before I did, and shut it. "Sit, Lily," he said. "Since you've gone to so much trouble, let's have a look at your work."

I fought to act normally, but had the horrible feeling that I wasn't being successful. I could hear my own voice scraping against the dryness in my throat. "Don't you think tomorrow would be better? It's late, and I've upset you. Anyway, I'm meeting someone soon. So—"

He stared at me, unblinking, his glasses seeming to magnify the ominous intensity of his gaze. "No, Lily. I insist. We need to have a talk, now."

I tried to tell myself that nothing was wrong. It was a coincidence; I was overwrought because of all that was happening to me. Scarabs were very common; there could have been others with the same inscription. It couldn't possibly be the one in my vision. There was no way that Dr. Briggs...

But there was, and it screamed at me even as I tried to argue against it. He had dated Cassandra Allingham. And Cassandra Allingham had been there when Amisihathor's tomb was opened. Wayward, beautiful, irresponsible Cassandra, who resented all the attention her parents devoted to Egyptology. It wouldn't have been too difficult to remove some small pieces and smuggle them out. No one would have suspected the young daughter of the esteemed archaeologists who had given so much to the Egyptian Museum. A double victory for her, spiting her parents and pleasing her lover. Perhaps it had even been his idea.

Was that how he had financed his career? I didn't want to believe it. But I knew in my heart who the scarab had belonged to. I could tell as soon as I saw it. And the way that Briggs was looking at me now as I mechanically took a chair sent shivers down my spine.

"The sketches, Lily," he said.

I handed them over silently. He viewed each one, lingering on the courtyard scene. Then, with a sudden, violent movement that made me jump, he bunched it up and threw it to the floor. "Blackmail is a very ugly activity," he said between clenched teeth. "Not to mention a dangerous one."

Is that what he thought I was doing? Surprise made my voice sound indignant. "What do you mean?" I demanded.

"Oh, come on. It's too late to play the innocent now. You get cozy with the Allinghams. Sketches are 'accidentally' left on your desk that show me you know what items from the tomb looked like, with those earrings right on top. I offer you a deal illustrating one of my books, but apparently that isn't enough for you. Now you come by with another drawing of an object that just happens to be in my desk drawer, which has always been kept under lock and key. Not very subtle, Lily. I get the message. You know. So what exactly do you want? It obviously can't be for the truth to come out. That would hurt Dame Ursula and your new boyfriend as much as it would me. And you'd never be able to prove anything. So I'm warning you. Take the book deal and be satisfied. With that and the Allingham connection, you'll be sitting pretty. Don't get too greedy, or you could spoil it all."

I was appalled. I had worked for this man for the past year, I had been proud of his prestige, and I had respected him. Now he was confessing to something I hadn't even imagined, but he didn't seem to feel any remorse. He was tarring me with his own brush as well. It stung to find that anyone could think of me as that kind of person. Nor did I appreciate being threatened. But I no longer knew whom I was dealing with, and I had to be careful.

"I was never looking for trouble, Dr. Briggs," I said. "I don't want Ursula or Kent to be hurt. But you should give back anything you still have from the tomb. The artifacts belong in

Egypt, along with the rest of Amisihathor's things. No one has to know where they came from. You of all people realize how important it is to have each and every artifact carefully studied."

"That's the party line, of course," he said with disdain. "But there are *much* more important things. Why should this work be shunted off to sit on a shelf in some museum, where there are so many objects, they can't possibly all be displayed and appreciated properly? These items were made for a *purpose,* and I have given that purpose back to them. I know their value and I treasure them each day. Their creators would approve."

"But they belong to the country of Egypt," I argued. "They're part of the heritage of all mankind."

"Well, I'm a part of mankind, aren't I?" he said, with a strange smile. "Most people could care less about our heritage. And why should a government over three thousand years later have a claim on something created by an individual who never dreamed they would exist? Was there a will that bequeathed it to them? I don't think so. The Egyptians robbed their own tombs from antiquity to the present day, destroying and plundering for profit. I have treated my finds with the respect and reverence that they deserve. I have utilized their power for the glory of ancient Egypt, not the satisfaction of some petty officials trying to rake in money from the tourist trade. 'Give us back our treasures'," he mocked. "'We had nothing to do with creating them, certainly did not preserve them, but we want them all here now, just so the world has to pay to come and see them!' No, Lily, they do not belong in Egypt. I am their guardian now, and I will never give them up."

The convoluted logic he had invented to justify what was plain and simple theft stunned me. In an academic of his stature, it was even more reprehensible. But I could see that I wouldn't get anywhere by contradicting him. All I wanted now was to escape. I felt overwhelmed, unable to deal with this sudden betrayal. I needed time to think. In what I hoped was a reasonable voice, I said, "Obviously, I can't force you to do anything. You're absolutely right. It had to be Cassandra who gave you those artifacts, and no one wants her family to be dragged into this. It would destroy them. So I won't say anything. Kent is too important to me."

"Very sensible of you, Lily. You hang onto that ticket, and there's no telling how far you can ride." He took the sketches and put them into his desk. "And watch what you draw more carefully, understand?"

"I understand." I stood up and walked towards the door. "Goodnight, Professor Briggs."

"Goodbye, Lily."

I held my breath until I was out of the office. Then I practically ran into the main hallway. There were few people about at this hour to notice my strange behavior. A woman sharing the elevator with me did ask if I was all right. I must have been as white as a sheet. When I was free of the building and in my car, I sat for some minutes simply staring into space. My mind could not process everything that had happened. Professor Briggs: a thief, a liar and a fraud. What on Earth was I going to do? I could not turn him in without hurting Kent and Ursula, and it was my word against his anyway. But if I said nothing, I was just as guilty as he was. One thing was certain either way; my job with him was over. I could never work with that man again. What it would mean to my academic career, I dared not think about now. I needed to find somewhere, some*one*, safe, to absorb this latest shock. But who? Kent was gone. Katy was out. My mother would only find a way to bring Stephen into it. And Stephen himself was another source of tension in my overwrought emotional life. So where could I find shelter?

In the end, I just went home. I wasn't in much of a state to do anything else. Craving comfort food, I surrendered to gluttony, and ate three pieces of my mother's pie, with ice cream piled on top. Then I had a candy bar for good measure. I was hardly surprised when I began feeling quite ill. I'll just take something and lie down, I thought to myself. I could decide what to do about Briggs tomorrow.

I swallowed some stomach medicine and curled up on the bed. Cleocatra, sensing my agitation, had been glued to me since I came in the door. Now she would not be quiet, pressing up against me and mewing loudly. "I'll be all right," I told her. "Just let me rest for a while."

It was hot in the room, but I didn't feel like getting up to check the air conditioning. I was hoping that if I didn't move, the pain beginning to knot up inside of me would go away. I tried to breathe deeply and focus on a peaceful mental image, the way I'd been taught in yoga class. I visualized a soft snow drifting down and icing the branches of trees, just like on a Christmas card. But something was wrong. The snow was melting. And the trees—they kept turning into palms. My white winter moon became a scorching summer sun. I began to tremble. Something was very wrong, and I was afraid.

Chapter Nineteen

Fear is something that I live with all of the time now. For Kahotep, for myself—and for Kamenwati. No matter how much I wish it were possible, I cannot bring myself to hate my husband. I realize that he is foul, destined for the mouth of Ammit, but when the pain of his betrayal tears at me, other images, unbidden and unwanted, spring up alongside of it. His face as he smiled at me for the first time. His strong, golden body, teaching me the meaning of delight. The tenderness in his voice as he promised that one day we would live together among the stars. I do not know which hurts me more.

Here in the House of Hathor, Kahotep has been kindness itself, but he cannot comfort me. I have learned that he suspects Kamenwati of taking bribes and stealing from the temple stores. My husband is far too clever to be caught, of course, but Kahotep has watched him closely, issuing many veiled threats. It is this, and Kamenwati's lust for power, that has spurred him to plot the priest's death. For three days now, investigations have been made and information gathered. I know that soon, Kamenwati's doom must fall. Kahotep will confront him, and he will be brought to court. Even now, I confess that I hope he will abandon Dendera. I would rather disgrace be his fate than death. Will Kepi run with him? I wonder bitterly. Will they cleave together in their shame? I have my doubts. Whatever they share, it cannot be love. And I do not think that lust will survive the poverty and humiliation that awaits them. I tell myself that Kamenwati deserves this, and much more. But I cannot bring myself to completely believe in this evil creature. Surely, he would not have actually sought the death of Kahotep. Not the man who sat beside me when I had a fever and put cool cloths to my brow. The man who had fashioned a doll from papyrus reeds for little Meretsankh. The man...

But I turn my mind firmly away from this well-worn path. There is no use in it. Kamenwati is lost to me, as surely as if he had been swallowed up by the sands of the desert. My only choice is to go forward, and live my life the best I can without him.

He has tried to reach me since I have been here. He has been told that I am in communion with the gods and cannot be disturbed. Does he suspect the peril that he is in? I certainly no longer believe that he would miss me for my own sake. He must have heard the whispers, noticed the unusual inquiries. Surely, he will run before he can be brought to judgment? I must accept that I will probably never see him again.

Blinking away my tears, I notice one of the temple cats, Bastet, walking towards me. As she reaches my legs, she winds herself around them. I reach down and stroke her silky fur. I have often fed her tidbits in the past, and she has stuck close to me these past days, as if sensing that I need comfort. I am grateful for her company. But now, she seems distressed. Her body is stiff and her eyes are snapping. "What is wrong, Bastet?" I ask soothingly. "Has someone been teasing you?"

She stares up, and a strange feeling seizes me. I almost expect to see her lips form words. Then she runs ahead, stops, and looks back. My skin tingles. Is the cat goddess herself trying to communicate with me through her sacred animal? I move towards her, and she runs again. She wants me to follow her. We are out in the temple garden, far from everyone. Therefore, I am surprised to see a child suddenly appear. It is a boy, still with his sidelock of youth, and he is calling out. "Mistress! Please! I have been sent to find you. I have a message!"

I stop and wait for him. Bastet hisses angrily. I continue following her, motioning to the child to accompany me. I recognize him as a scribe in training who attends the temple school. He reaches me at last and, panting, thrusts a piece of papyrus into my hand. I reward him with a turquoise bead, and he scampers off happily. Breaking the seal, I open up the papyrus. My feet stop in their tracks, for it is signed with Kamenwati's name. Suddenly, my hand is shaking. My eyes rake over the message.

'My dearest wife. Why do you absent yourself so long from me, with no word to comfort? I would that you had shared with me the dreams that have so concerned you. The days and nights

are long without your presence. You must know that I am thinking of you, for never did a man love a woman more. Remember all we have been to each other, and send me a sign. Your Kamenwati.'

The ink seems to swim before my eyes. I stand as one in a fever, paying no attention to Bastet swiping her paw at the hem of my dress. How does he dare? How does he dare to write to me as if he had never planned to put me aside? As if, even now, his doom were not swooping in upon him? Did he think I would lift a finger to help him, even if it were in my power? Foolish Kamenwati! But even as my heart rages, this visible reminder of my husband cuts me to the quick. 'Remember all we have been to each other.' As if I could forget! I know that I should destroy this piece of deceit and scatter its shreds to the wind. Why, then, do I find myself rolling it up and inserting it into the cylinder around my neck? There is room in there with my oracular decree. When I return to my chamber in the temple, I will take it out and dispose of it. After I am able to gather my thoughts more carefully.

When at last I look up, Bastet has disappeared. I begin my walk back, but suddenly, a noise like the whole sky being torn apart assails my ears. For a moment, I am dumbfounded; then, I very slowly turn around, my body trembling. The sight that greets me paralyzes me with terror. A great wave of swirling, howling dust is ripping across the desert towards me. It blots out the boat of Ra and moves with the speed of the Nile flood. A sandstorm! And I am far from the safety of any walls. I break into a frantic run, knowing that my only hope is to reach the temple buildings. I pray desperately as my feet fly. As despondent as I have been, I do not want to die! So much may yet happen, another chance for me to know happiness, to lead a different kind of life. I must have a chance! But even as I strain every part of my being, the merciless storm is bearing down upon me. I can feel its stinging bite on my skin. The ground is churning beneath me, trapping my sandals. I can no longer make any headway against the ferocious wind. With a sob of despair, I sink down onto my knees. The whole world is now a raging, choking mass of sand. It is tearing through me, stealing my *breath. An image of Kahotep comes into my mind. Every act of care and kindness that he has ever shown me I see again in an instant. His was a true love, a selfless love, and I never understood how priceless that was. If only I could tell him! But it is too late! I am alone, all alone. Oh, my love, forgive me. I did not realize! Will I see you in the afterlife now? Will you take my hand and smile at me?*

Beloved, be with me. Mistress, welcome me into the western mountain. Let maat prevail…

I am floating. Am I on air or water? My body has no weight, and I can actually see my mind, a bright cloud of light, floating along beside it. My body and mind mix, swirl together, and separate again. What shape would words take, I wonder? I try a few, but I sense that they are not leaving my mouth, and I don't have enough breath to utter them. Yet someone responds. They put a mask over my face and hook something into my arm. Then the voices are drowned out by the chattering of birds in the trees. I am in a lush garden filled with sweet scents. A beautiful flower floating on the surface of a green pool captures my attention. It has large, soft petals that glow with an unearthly blue light. I watch it, entranced. Suddenly, it speaks to me in a musical, feminine voice. *"You cannot stay here,"* it says.

I am pierced by sadness. "Why not?" I ask.

"Your story is not over, my sister. You must return, and speak for both of us. Then we may continue to live. I know that you are tired. But you must not give in. Have courage, and all will be well. Open your eyes."

My lids flickered. I heard the sound of sobbing. The sight of my unemotional mother with tears streaming down her face gave me a real shock. I must be dying, I thought in horror. She would never be looking like that if I weren't. My eyes drifted around the bed and I saw Stephen and Kent. But neither one of them noticed me. All their attention was focused on my mother, and I felt the irony that she had somehow managed to take the spotlight. I can't even star in my own death, I thought peevishly. They each had one of her arms and were leading her out of the room. I was going to protest, but I could not summon the strength. White clad figures bustled about me. One was waving his finger in front of my face. I watched it go by, and he said, "Pupils are responsive! Lily! Lily, can you hear me?"

The answer seemed to be very important, so I summoned all my strength and licked my dry lips. I wasn't sure whether or not I croaked "Yes" out loud, but it seemed the owner of the finger was satisfied. He barked out some orders and various instruments swung into action. I only cared about the cold cloths placed on my skin. It was very hot. Why did they have the heat on so high? I longed for a cool breeze. Or a cool drink…

Kent reappeared momentarily beside me, leaning over and kissing my forehead. "I love you," he whispered. Stephen came back too. "You're going to be all right, kid," he said. "Just hang in there." I did not want them to go. I suddenly felt terribly alone. Why was everyone leaving? Who was going to make sure that I was safe?

"*I am, Princess.*"

My father was standing smiling at me. He was just the way I remembered him, and I was filled with joy. "Daddy!" I cried, throwing my arms around him. I was so happy I wept, and he hugged me with all the warmth and love that had made me feel so secure in childhood. I did not have to say a word, for I knew that he understood everything in my heart. For a space that was timeless, I simply drew comfort and strength from him. Then, just as I had when I was a little girl, I fell asleep in his embrace.

I was safe.

Chapter Twenty

The next time I awoke, Kent was sitting on the side of the bed and Stephen was standing over me, checking a chart. I blinked lazily. On the edge of my vision, I could see vases of flowers and a smiley-faced balloon. The awful sense of burning was gone, and its absence was bliss. I simply wanted to enjoy it, but I felt compelled to speak and reassure them. "Hi," I said.

They both smiled and said, "Hi!" at the same time, only Stephen added, "honey" and Kent added "love." There was an instant of embarrassed silence, and then Stephen spoke again. "How are you feeling?" he asked.

"Better. Much better. I'm thirsty. Can I have a drink?"

"Sure." They both moved towards the pitcher of water on the table. Seeing imminent disaster, I said quickly, "I'd really like some milk."

They looked at each other uncertainly, neither wanting to be the one to leave. Finally, Kent pushed the call button. Then he took my hand in both of his. "It's brilliant to see you back," he said, and the relief in his eyes almost hurt, it was so intense.

Stephen sat down on the other side of the bed and took my left hand, giving it a squeeze. "I couldn't be any happier," he stated sincerely.

I felt like a human wishbone between them. "Am I—am I all right now?" I asked awkwardly.

"Oh, yes!" said Stephen assuredly. "Most of the toxin is gone from your system. It's simply a matter of time until your body's recovered from the ordeal."

"The ordeal of *what*?" I asked. "What was wrong with me?"

"Sweetheart—" Kent paused, seemingly unable to find words. I was surprised to see him look at Stephen as if ceding him the right to speak further; and it was Stephen who answered me. "I'm sorry to have to tell you this, kid," he said. "I know what a shock it's going to be. But you have to know, and I think you're strong enough. What happened to you is, in a nutshell— you were poisoned."

Even now, my befuddled brain could not take in the full impact of his statement. "What? You mean like carbon monoxide?"

"I mean, like a toxic alkaloid," Stephen said grimly. "A small amount would make you feel tired, headachy, and disoriented. But it wouldn't be fatal or even do any permanent damage. Some people are more sensitive though, and things can get nasty. Larger doses can cause fever, rapid heartbeat, difficulty breathing—even death."

"But where did I get it?" I asked in bewilderment. "Was it something I ate?"

Kent squeezed my hand tightly, while Stephen replied, "Yes, it was something you ate. But it was given to you."

"Dr. Briggs!" I gasped, realization flooding over me. "Oh, my God! All of those snacks at work. Or was it in the coffee? He thought I was going to tell. He would rather have killed me than lose my career. That bastard! But I wouldn't have done it to you and Ursula, Kent, not without talking to you first. I really wouldn't."

Both men were looking at me in concern. Kent made soothing noises while Stephen checked my pulse and felt my forehead. "Maybe this can wait until later," he said. "You're still recovering, and you need to rest. Just lie still, honey. Take some deep breaths. You'll be fine, don't worry."

"But have they arrested him yet?" I demanded. "Did they get the things he stole from the tomb?" I looked at Kent. "I'm sure he'll make some kind of deal. It doesn't have to come out, what your mother did. You'd better go to the police and see what you can do."

Again, a strange glance between the two men. Stephen nodded slightly, then got up and left the room. Kent said, "Don't think about anything now, love. You're safe. That's all that matters."

"The hell it is!" I answered indignantly. "He's got to be locked up! Have they arrested him, or not?"

"Peter Briggs?" asked Kent with maddening obtuseness.

"Yes! He's the one who did this to me! He thought he could bribe me with the book, and then with blackmail. I told him I wouldn't say anything, but he obviously decided it wasn't worth the risk." Suddenly, I burst into tears. "He never really wanted my illustrations at all!"

I sobbed away as if this was the worst aspect of the whole affair. Kent tried to gather me into his arms, but he accidentally pulled on my IV. I howled louder than ever.

"What's going on here?" Stephen had re-entered the room with a doctor in tow. It was the latter who asked the question while glaring suspiciously at Kent.

"She just started crying. She's upset about Dr. Briggs. I think I may have loosened her line, I'm sorry." Kent moved back as the doctor took center stage and began fussing over me. After a brief examination and a few questions, he spoke to Stephen as if Kent and I didn't even exist.

"She's just a little dehydrated; blood pressure's a bit on the high side. Nothing unexpected. The mental and emotional confusion will go away in a day or so. She's very lucky that she had you on hand."

"Thank you, Doctor." For an absurd moment, I wondered if Stephen was going to salute. Then Doctor Obnoxious glided off into the sunset. I used half a box of tissue blowing my nose and trying to be coherent again. Kent obligingly moved the wastebasket within my reach, while Stephen gazed at me with a paternal air.

"Did you hear that, Lily? You're going to be as right as rain. I told you there was nothing to worry about. These feelings and outbursts are completely normal. It's all part of the recovery process."

"Isn't wanting my attempted murderer to be arrested completely normal, too?" I sniffled. "Why doesn't anyone seem to care about that?"

"Because we don't know what you're talking about, love," said Kent. Stephen frowned at him.

"Remember, Lily," he interrupted, "your mind is still playing tricks on you. Try to let it go, accept it's only a symptom, and relax. You don't have to think about anything now."

"Will you stop treating me as if I'm brain damaged?" I nearly shouted. "I know what I—" and I stopped suddenly as an awful truth hit me like a tidal wave. "Or am I?" I gasped. "Brain damaged?" My eyes filled with tears once more. "Oh no, please tell me—"

"There is nothing wrong with your brain," said Kent loudly and firmly. "Don't cry, my love. Just tell me what happened with Dr. Briggs."

"This isn't—" Stephen began, but Kent ignored him and cupped my chin in his hand. "Go slowly. Remember that I don't know anything about this story. Start from the beginning, and take your time."

I remembered myself enough to say to Stephen, "Can you leave us alone, please? This is something personal about Kent's family."

Stephen looked daggers at Kent, but spoke to me. "You should not be doing this, Lily. You should be resting. I don't approve of this at all."

"Well, you're not in charge, are you?" Kent replied mildly. "So run along like a good chap. It's obvious that Lily *can't* rest until she gets this off her chest."

"Please, Stephen," I repeated. "I'm all right. This is important."

"I'm going to be outside the door," he said, through clenched teeth. "And I'm going to be checking on you."

Kent muttered something underneath his breath, but turned to me expectantly when Stephen was gone. "All right, love. Go ahead."

So I did. I recounted the entire meeting between Briggs and me—whatever night it had been. By now, I'd lost all track of time. I tried to break the news of Cassandra's complicity as gently as I could, but considering the state I was in, it wasn't the most tactful job. When I was finished, Kent got up, his face stricken, and went to stand at the window. He stared out of it silently, trying to master his emotions.

"I'm sorry," I said softly. "I wish I had never had to tell you. But we've got to stop him."

Kent turned back around to look at me. "Yes," he agreed in a choked voice. "Yes. He's got to be dealt with. But I need time, Lily. I have to talk to Gram, and Philip, and think about what to do. Will you give me that time?"

I couldn't believe what I was hearing. Was he actually requesting that Briggs' arrest be delayed? Was his mother's reputation more important than my attempted murder? I opened my mouth to speak, then closed it again, unable to utter a word. Kent stepped towards me, a pleading expression on his face, and at that moment, Stephen came bursting back into the room. "I've got your milk, Lily," he said, brandishing the carton triumphantly. "Do you want to drink it now?"

I could feel the sob rising up in my throat. "I want to be alone," I said shakily. "Both of you, go."

Stephen shot an apprehensive glance at me and a murderous one at Kent. "But, honey— " he began. I squeezed my eyes shut. "Go, now!" I cried, and buried my head in the pillow.

I could hear their low, angry voices muttering as they left, but the words were lost to me as my tears began flowing. No one was taking me seriously. Stephen treated me like a confused child, and Kent was willing to let my attacker wander around free. Briggs could be escaping at this very moment. I felt utterly abandoned. A nurse came in to check on me and I sobbed out loud, "I want my Mom!"

"I'm sorry, Miss Evans. Your mother isn't here right now. Is there anything I can do for you?"

Not here! How could she not be here? My own mother, leaving me at a time like this! My misery was complete. "No one cares!" I moaned.

The nurse replied soothingly, "Of course they do! I know this has been a terrible ordeal, but you've come through it now. Everything will be better tomorrow, you'll see. By then, you can have a phone in your room, and you'll be able to talk to all the people who have been calling to check on you. We can start letting in visitors outside of the family as well. Remember, you're not going to be thinking clearly right now, and that's nothing to worry about. Go easy on yourself. You're recovering.

Why don't you just try to rest? Take a drink—that's right. Good. Would you like me to stay for a while?"

"No, thank you," I replied faintly. "I just want to sleep."

"That's the best thing for you. Push the button if you need anything."

And suddenly, I was too tired to even cry any more. Any further thought or action was going to have to wait. I closed my eyes, and a dream I had had tugged at the edge of my mind. A smile, warmth, a feeling of love so powerful that it dispelled the pain like the sun banishes mist. Disjointed images floated across my consciousness. My father. A middle-aged Egyptian man with a face full of dignity and kindness. A beautiful blue flower. I was falling down into sleep, and I surrendered myself to it.

Chapter Twenty-one

I passed a night mercifully free of any dreams. So deep was my sleep that I was not even aware of the medical checks. The blood draw early the next morning put a stop to that, however. It is hard not to notice a needle probing around in search of a vein. Once that grisly business had been conducted, I attempted to eat the breakfast they put before me. I wasn't sure exactly what it was, but it reminded me of the gruel that was given to Oliver Twist. I pushed the spoon around in it listlessly, then drank some of the hot tea on the tray. The staff had decided that it would be good for me to get out of bed. While simple in theory, in practice it involved about the same amount of energy that would be needed to climb Mount Everest. I took two steps, then turned right back around. "Very good!" my day nurse said encouragingly. "Later on, you can sit for a while in the chair."

I hoped so. I didn't like lying helplessly with everyone looking down at me. But for now, I had no choice. I was exhausted. "Has Dr. Mallory been in touch today?" I asked, as I settled back on my pillows.

"Oh, yes. In fact, he looked in while you were still asleep. He said he'd be back by eleven."

Good. I was determined to get some answers out of Stephen. "And do you know if my phone is working yet?"

The nurse checked it, and shook her head. "I'm afraid not. Did someone arrange to have it turned on?"

"I don't know." This was very aggravating. I felt cut off from the whole world.

"I'm sure someone will see to it." She poured me a glass of water from the pitcher on my table. "Why don't you try some of this. The more you drink, the sooner we can get you off the IV."

I swallowed a few sips dutifully, glancing at the clock. Visiting hours were almost due to start. Where were my mother and Kent? Did they have higher priorities than seeing about me? I was feeling very sorry for myself when a welcome face appeared at the door.

"Katy!" I exclaimed.

My friend rushed over and gave me a hug. "Oh, Lily, you don't know how glad I am to see you! I've been *so* worried! Thank God you're all right. How do you feel today?"

"Better. There was really no place to go but up." I smiled faintly.

"Everyone is asking about you. Did you see the flowers we sent?" Without waiting for an answer, Katy opened up the bag she was carrying. "I stopped by your place and got you some things." She set some toiletries on the bedside table, then produced my favorite photo of my father. "And here's your own pillow. Thought you'd like that." A few items of clothing she placed in a drawer. "I would have smuggled Cleo in for a visit, but she isn't exactly the type to come quietly."

"Who's looking after her?" I asked anxiously. "Is she at Mom's?"

"No." Katy turned away to put my slippers on the floor. "Stephen's got her. They'll probably be giving interviews on the six o'clock news. I hope your TV's turned on."

"What do you mean?" I demanded, and she looked at me in surprise. "Don't you know?" she asked. "I mean, what Stephen did?"

"No," I replied, staring at her. "I can't remember much of anything."

"Well." Katy leaned forward importantly. "He called you on Friday night. The phone was picked up, but no one answered. All he could hear was Cleo yowling. He said it sounded so unearthly that it sent chills down his spine. He was worried that something was wrong, and drove over to your apartment. He saw your car, but when you didn't come to the door, he went inside. He found you unconscious on your bed. The phone was still off the hook. We reckon that Cleo swiped it with her paw. The two of them saved your life."

I let out a long breath. "Wow," I said, with total inadequacy.

"Wow, indeed. I guess I'll never be able to criticize Stephen again. But, still, your Kent is fabulous too. I can see why you flipped for him. He was just like a knight in shining armor. Oh, those gorgeous eyes! It's simply not fair for a man to have those long charcoal lashes."

"Where did you run into Kent?" I asked in confusion. "Is he outside? I haven't seen him yet today."

"Well, I don't suppose you will, until he gets out of jail," said Katy practically.

I put my head in my hands. "Stop!" I begged. "I don't understand! *What* are you talking about?"

For the first time, Katy looked nonplussed. "You really haven't heard about any of this? Gosh, Lily, I hope it's all right for me to tell you. Maybe we should wait—"

I fixed her with a steely gaze. "Katy Morrison," I said firmly, "you will explain everything to me, right now."

Concern and the desire to burst out with the information warred on Katy's elfin face. "Don't worry," I assured her impatiently, "you won't kill me. But I may kill you if you don't spill it."

Being thus absolved, Katy leaned forward eagerly. "Well, I took the day off to come and be with you. I went to your apartment, and then I stopped by work to print off an important letter. I had just finished when in walks a tall dark stranger. He looks at me and asks if I'm Katy Morrison, and when I hear his accent, I know who he must be. Sure enough, he introduces himself and shakes my hand. Such lovely manners! I figured he had come to talk about you. But he wanted me to show him where Dr. Briggs' office was. I took him down the hall to the great man's den. The door was shut, but you could hear him moving around in there. 'Thank you,' says Kent. 'Now will you ring the local police and have them come over here? And if you'd be so kind, this is my solicitor's number. I expect he'll be needing to bail me out'.

"I could tell by the look on his face that he wasn't joking. Still, I didn't actually call the cavalry until the shouting started. We all tried to listen, of course, but the office is pretty far away. I heard snatches about artifacts and mothers and you, Lily, with various obscenities thrown in. Mostly Briggs' voice. Then some thuds and crashes. Someone must have notified security because they came busting in like the Earps at the OK Corral. Poor little

McKenzie was bringing up the rear. You remember, the one who helped you when you locked the keys in the car? He's never been involved in anything more serious than a parking violation. If you could have seen how terrified he looked, your heart would have bled for him. Still, he did his duty, I've got to give him credit—"

"Katy!" I said through clenched teeth.

"Sorry. But there's so much to tell! Anyway, they crouched down outside of the office and yelled, 'Break it up in there! Come out with your hands up!' I never thought I'd hear that in real life. Nothing happened for a minute. Then the door opened and Kent and Briggs came tumbling out, still tangling with each other. Briggs' glasses were gone and he was bleeding. It was all over Kent's shirt. Briggs was panting, 'Arrest this man! He's assaulting me!' And Kent was saying, 'Arrest *this* man. He's a thief and a blackmailer!' Security pulled them off of each other and hustled them away until the police came. I did call the lawyer, so I'm sure Kent will be free soon. I know he must have been defending your honor somehow, but of course, if it's too emotional right now, I don't want you to tell me about it."

She meant it, too. I had never appreciated her friendship more than I did at that moment, knowing how insatiably curious she must be, but willing to wait if explanations would upset me. I wished I could put her out of her misery. "It's a long story, Katy, and not really mine to tell. But it makes me very happy to know that Kent did that. Briggs is a terrible man who hurt Kent's family, then tried to get me to hush it up. It's the whole reason he poisoned me. I'm surprised that he didn't run, but I guess his reputation is so damn precious to him, he actually thought he'd get away with it. Thank God he's finally in jail where he belongs."

Katy looked confused, and I didn't blame her. But I couldn't say any more until I had talked to Kent. "Maybe I should get a lawyer myself," I mused. "Will you do me a favor, and go to the patient office and make sure the telephone gets turned on? I can't stand being so out of touch."

"Sure," Katy agreed. "I'll do that right now."

She left with such alacrity that I wondered if I'd upset her. But I couldn't tell the whole truth without Kent's permission. As soon as I could communicate, I would call his mobile to make sure he was all right. And then I would check on my mother. I was worried that my troubles had so upset her that she had had to be put to bed. Perhaps all those maladies I had listened to with only half an ear were more serious than I realized. Voices in the hallway distracted me from these guilty thoughts. I recognized them as Katy's and Stephen's. They were too low for me to understand, but the conversation lasted long enough for me to know that Katy really had changed her opinion of him. She never would have had so much to say to Stephen before.

After a few minutes, he was in the room, smiling at me. "How are you feeling today, kid? You have a lot more color. I hear you were able to get out of bed."

"It wasn't *my* idea," I replied, "but I lived. I'm mainly just tired, and sore. How can lying around do such a number on your muscles?"

"That will be dehydration, and mineral loss. Nothing the IV won't cure. Drink as much as you can. That will help more than anything."

"Stephen," I said, feeling suddenly shy, "Katy was telling me what happened. I don't quite know how to say thank you. You saved my life."

He sat down on the bed beside me, and a strange look came over his face. "You know, Lily, it's a funny thing." He paused, and I waited expectantly. Stephen had always been a very practical man, not given to flowery language or displays of emotion. I had no idea what he was going to say, but I was still shocked when I heard it.

"I had to be up very early Saturday morning, so I was asleep by nine o'clock Friday night. Remember how odd you used to think it was that I never remembered my dreams?"

I nodded. He was a very sound sleeper, and claimed that he didn't dream at all. I said that everyone did, but some people just didn't recall them. When I was irritated with him, I used to wonder if this was due to the fact that he didn't have any imagination.

"Well, I had one hell of a nightmare. I was standing beside your body. You were dressed like an ancient Egyptian, but it was you. You were lying in the sand, and the sand was trying to suck you in. I grabbed hold of your arms and pulled, but I wasn't strong enough. You were getting dragged down. First your feet, then your legs—it was swallowing you whole." He gave an involuntary shudder, then continued.

"Finally, there was nothing left but your head. I was afraid that you were dead. But then your eyes opened, and your lips moved. 'Help me!' you said. God, it was awful. There was sand coming out of your mouth. And a cat was crouched there, too, howling like a demon. I was so relieved when I woke up. But the dream stayed with me, like a weight pressing down. At last, I got up and decided that I had to see if you were okay. I called, and the phone clicked like you had picked it up, but you didn't say anything. All I could hear was Cleo yowling. It sounded just like the cat in my dream. I knew I couldn't rest until I talked to you. I drove over to your place, cursing myself for a fool the whole time. I saw your car, but there were no lights on, and you didn't come to the door. Before I even knew it, I was running inside. I found you on the bed. Your pulse was so rapid, I was afraid..." He shook himself mentally, and came back to the present. "But here you are, safe and sound. So, do you think I'm crazy now?"

In answer, I put both of my arms around him. "I think you're absolutely wonderful," I whispered, tears of gratitude on my cheeks. And I silently thanked Amisihathor for sending him.

We held each other for a few minutes in a comforting embrace. Then I told him the rest of Katy's news. "They've arrested Dr. Briggs. Kent turned him in a while ago. The other charges were serious enough, but poisoning should get him put away for quite a few years."

Stephen sighed and released me. Instead of relief, I saw sadness on his face. "What?" I asked, feeling a new knot of fear in my stomach.

"Honey, there's something I've got to tell you. I don't know exactly what crimes Briggs has committed, but poisoning is not one of them."

"But you said—you said that it was deliberate. You said the poison was put into my food."

"It was. But not by someone who really wanted to hurt you. She thought you'd feel unwell, but she never dreamed it would almost kill you. You've got to believe that, Lily."

"She? Stephen! Who is *she*?" I demanded.

He hesitated, then said quietly, "Your mother."

Chapter Twenty-two

For a full minute, I stared at him, uncomprehending. Then I shook my head, and I went on shaking it, violently. "No," I said, and in case he didn't understand, I said it again. "No!"

"Honey, listen." He stilled my movement by taking my face in his hands. "You've got to accept this. She didn't realize how dangerous it would be. All she wanted was for you to decide that your life was too stressful, that having Kent in it was making you sick. She thought you'd turn to me if you didn't feel well, and that would bring us closer together. So she added a few toxic berries to a pie. If you'd only eaten one piece, it wouldn't have come to this, but you ingested much more than she intended. She really had no idea of the harm she was doing, or that you'd have such a sensitivity to the alkaloid. She didn't want you to marry Kent and go off to England. She's a troubled woman, Lily, and she needs help. I'm not trying to defend her, but I know that in her own twisted way, she believed she was acting for your own good."

"Is that what she told you?" I was full of so much hurt, anger, and pain that I thought it might choke me. "That she was doing me a *favor*?"

"Of course not. She was horrified when she saw what she'd done. They took her away for a psychiatric evaluation. She's here in the hospital now."

My mind reeled in despair. What more was there for me to endure? Was there no end to this nightmare?

Stephen rubbed my back as if I was a child. "I'm so sorry," he said gently. "I know what a blow this is. I think you might want to talk to a professional about it. There's an excellent doctor on staff here— "

"Oh, good!" I exclaimed, my voice rising dangerously high. "Maybe he can treat my mother *and* me! Kill two birds with one stone!"

He did not reply, but instead, he poured me a cup of water. "Drink," he urged, and I did, automatically. "Now take a deep breath. That's right. And another one. Remember the most important thing, Lily. You are alive. You are going to get well. And you are incredibly strong. You've handled everything that's happened to you, and you'll be able to handle this." He tilted up my chin and locked his eyes with mine. "And you're not alone."

I sucked in my sobs, and nodded. I could not afford to deal with this right now. I had to push it away or it would overwhelm me. "Thank you," I gulped. "If you don't mind, I think I need some time alone."

"Sure. I'll tell Katy to come back later. And you know that all you have to do is call me."

I nodded again, and Stephen's lips brushed across mine. "I'll see you soon, honey," he said, and left.

I stared off into space for a minute, trying to make my mind a blank. Then I turned on the TV for a numbing distraction. I watched cartoons until I was almost in a trance. I didn't even see the door open, and didn't notice Kent until he put himself between the screen and me. "Hello, love," he said, almost apologetically. "Do you feel up to a visit?"

The sight of him shook me out of my self-absorption. He looked terrible. His face was lined with worry and fatigue, and an ugly yellow bruise was spreading across his jaw. I held out my hand to him in a rush of compassion. "Oh, Kent! Come here and tell me what's happened! Katy said that you've been in jail!"

"True." He shuffled over and sat down beside me. "I must say, I'm done in. But what about you? How do you feel?"

"Horrible," I said, honestly. "But I want to hear *your* story. You're not in any trouble, are you? You didn't get arrested?"

"No." He sighed. "I went voluntarily. Briggs wanted me done for assault and slander, but I told the police that I was assisting them in apprehending a criminal. I don't know which one of us they believed, if either. It's been left to our defenders to sort out. Both of us have been released, but strongly cautioned not to leave the area. I had no intention of doing that, anyway."

As curious as I was about the showdown with Briggs, there was still the mystery of Kent's previous disappearance. "Why did you have to leave before?" I asked. "It sounded serious, and I was really worried. I couldn't find out anything. I still don't know what the emergency was, or how it came out."

"I'm sorry. More deep dark secrets, I'm afraid. My God, I can't believe how many of them are lurking in our lives. This one is Philip's. He's married, you see. She's a former flamenco dancer who snared him one night when he got drunk in a club. Poor old Phil. His one and only act of abandon, and it got him shackled to this harpy from hell. She won't divorce him. When he first brought it up to her, she checked herself into a very exclusive private facility and had a 'complete breakdown'. He gives in to outrageous demands to keep her out of our lives. She's been in Spain for the past year, but last week, we got a call that she was in the London house swanning about like the Queen of Sheba. I went over with Philip to help sort her out. We didn't want Gram to know, but she found out anyway and insisted on coming as well. To make a long story short, we all finally just decided that enough was enough. It's horrible to live with things being held over your head. What passes for peace can have too high a price. It will be unpleasant, and scandal is taken more seriously in England, but we won't have any more secrets. Not about her, nor about Mum."

"You all decided to confront Briggs," I said quietly. Now that I knew attempted murder had never been part of the picture, I admired their courage. It would have been easier to hush it up, deal with it privately, yet they had not taken the easy path. "You have a lot of character, Kent Ashton."

"I don't know." He sounded so tired, so sad, that my heart ached for him. "I was half out of my mind with worry. When I got back on Friday night, I went to your apartment. The lady next door saw me standing there and came running out, all agog with the news that you'd been taken away to hospital. I rushed over and they told me that you were having GI decontamination, and you were in serious condition. When I went to the emergency waiting room, I recognized your mum from the pictures at your place. The insufferable Stephen—sorry, I know he saved your life, and I'm forever grateful, but—he was with her. I introduced myself and they greeted me like I was Jack the Ripper. 'This is all your fault!' says she. I was gobsmacked. You having to drink liquid charcoal? All my fault? What would you have thought?"

I couldn't help but smile. "Poor Kent. You thought I'd tried to do away with myself because of you."

"Well, not really," he said sheepishly. "But it was hard to think straight, I was that upset. *Why* hadn't I called you? Why hadn't I told you I was coming back? Why hadn't I been here to prevent it somehow? I was torturing myself when Stephen said 'Lily has been poisoned. It's built up in her bloodstream and her system has gone into shock.' 'What do you mean?' I demanded. 'What kind of poison?'

"It was at that moment the doctors came out to tell us they were going to move you upstairs. Stephen and your mother went in to see you and I followed them. Your mum was muttering something but I couldn't understand her. All of my attention was on you, lying there, looking so—"

He didn't seem to want to, nor to be able to dwell on that, and he continued quickly with the story.

"Suddenly, your mum started to cry. 'I didn't mean it! I didn't know! I only used a little! My baby! Oh God, don't tell me I did this!' She was trying to hug you and making the most horrible noise. Everyone thought she was hysterical, and the doctors asked us to take her away. Stephen and I each grabbed one of her arms, and when we got out into the hall, she simply collapsed. He was holding her up and she was admitting to him that she'd put some kind of berry into your food. 'I just wanted her to marry you and stay here, Stephen!' she was sobbing. He put her into a chair and then he rang the psychiatric chaps. I went back in to check on you, and they said you had responded and that was very encouraging. After that, I just sat in the waiting room until you fell into a natural sleep. That was when you were pronounced out of danger, and as Stephen was glued to your side and could be of more use, I went to the house and slept for a few hours. I didn't think I'd be able to close my eyes, but I was so shattered, it was hours before I opened them. I came back the next morning, and that was when you told us about Briggs."

"I thought he was the one who poisoned me," I said tremulously. "I didn't know—"

Kent slipped an arm around me, and our heads rested together. "Our mothers surprised us both," he said with typical British understatement.

"What did Ursula say?" I questioned him. "It must have been a terrible blow to her."

"Do you know, I don't believe she was really surprised." Kent's voice took on a reflective tone. "I tried to go about it delicately, asking if she'd noticed things missing from the tomb. 'Something was always missing,' she said. 'In those days, it was often the officials who took items, so what could one say? They belonged to Egypt, after all.' So I pressed further to see if she could name any in particular. She told me of an ivory scarab with an inscription on it. When she saw the look on my face, she demanded to know why I was asking. 'Lily has seen that in Peter Briggs' office,' I said.

"She was quiet for a while. Then she started talking about Mum. She never said a bad word while I was growing up. She let me keep the fantasy of glamorous parents who were so important that the world needed them. The truth was that both were shallow people who needed excitement to feel alive. Regular jobs, a permanent home, raising children: those things weren't exciting. They were always chasing the bright lights. Gram quite calmly stated that Mum must have stolen the figures and given them to Peter Briggs, because she was jealous that the excavation took so much of Gram's time and attention. 'I did try to be a good mother,' she told me, 'but somehow I failed. I got a second chance with you boys. Now you're grown up, and all I have to be preoccupied with is the ghost of an ancient Egyptian girl.'

"It was gutting to see her look so sad. Of course, I told her that she hadn't failed, that Mum was responsible for her own choices. And I believe that. Remember, Lily? Guilt is the cruelest emotion. And the most self-indulgent."

I knew he was pointing this out to me, too. "So Ursula—and Philip? —agreed that you should confront Briggs," I said.

"All of us want to be free from the past," Kent replied. "And he couldn't be allowed to get away with treating you as he did. No blackmail. Of course, it's going to have to be proved that he possesses stolen antiquities. He's hidden them somewhere, and he won't admit it. There's an unholy mess ahead. But I know we did the right thing. As long as you're well, everything else will sort itself out."

An unholy mess. Yes, that was an apt description. Would it ever be sorted out? I wondered wearily. Tears began leaking from my eyes. "Oh, Kent," I moaned, "what am I going to do about my mother?"

He held me as best he could in the awkward hospital bed. "You're going to realize that she is a sick woman, help her get treatment, and keep on loving her even through your hatred, I expect," he said.

Somehow, he made it possible to mourn without feeling crushed by the emotion. I knew he was mourning too, and our grief flowed together. A nurse came in, looked, and had the decency to go away. All the time, the noise of the cartoons droned on incongruously in the background.

Chapter Twenty-three

That evening, I received a call from Dame Ursula. I thanked her for the huge bouquet of gorgeous flowers she had sent, and answered her solicitous questions concerning my health. I was wondering uneasily whether I should mention Peter Briggs when Ursula, in her usual forthright manner, solved the dilemma for me. "I don't want you to berate yourself in any way, Lily," she said. "You were an innocent party in an old, sad drama."

"But," I protested, "if it wasn't for me, none of this would be happening."

"And you think that would be a good thing?" asked Ursula gently. "My dear, I have always been aware of my daughter's faults. Understand, she was not a bad person. She just lived in the moment, and never really considered the consequences. She was very young, and head over heels in love with Peter Briggs. I think it was a desire to impress him that triggered her actions as much as a rebellion against me. I believe the theft was her only true crime. For the rest, being an absentee mother was the worst of it. It saddens me to think what joy she missed, not spending more time with Philip and Kent. But nothing can touch her now. And it's right that Peter should be taken to account for his actions. Who knows what else he has withheld from the world? Hoarding knowledge for personal gain is a very great sin in archaeology. Clearly, he has no scruples. Even if he cannot be convicted of theft, it should be known that he has done this. He has no right to be teaching others when he is such a bad example."

Her words made sense, but I still wasn't satisfied. "I hate it that your family will have to deal with the fall-out, though. It's bad enough that Philip's wife is causing trouble, without the scandal of the tomb being raked up."

"Do you know, Lily, it's actually a relief to me that Philip is facing down that dreadful woman, at last. No matter what ridiculous stories she tells the press or what kinds of scenes she makes, he won't be beholden to her any longer. I won't pretend

I'll welcome the publicity, but I'm tougher than those sweet boys give me credit for. My career has been long and fulfilling, and no one can take that away from me. I believe my work speaks for itself. I hope no one will hold their mother's mistakes against Kent or Philip. But I know that they feel this has to be faced. Then they will be free to move on. We all have to do what we feel is right, dear. If we do that, and care for each other, I think at the end of the day, we may not judge ourselves too harshly."

I thought of these words later as I lay watching the city lights outside my window. I had been able to eat some dinner and drink enough that the IV was gone from my arm. Although I was exhausted, my mind seemed to be working with unusual clarity. To do what was right, and not merely what made us happy, was the ultimate test of character. I reflected on Ursula, Kent, and Stephen. I considered my mother, even though the pain was still so raw that I had to force my mind not to shy away. I would be well soon, and it would be up to me to take care of her. Forgiveness might be a long way off, but she needed me. Kent was right. I would keep loving her through my hatred. And I had to consider what kind of affect his presence in my life would have on her recovery. Also, if it was fair to have Stephen so involved. I would have to make important decisions soon, not least concerning my work. How would my position change now? All I knew was that things would be very different. Would I be finishing my degree on schedule, or concentrating more on my art? Whatever happened, my story was just beginning.

But there was someone else whose story had nearly ended. I closed my eyes, and thought of Amisihathor. Her voice had become so familiar in my head, I believed that I could conjure it up. I summoned the peace I had felt in my last dreams, the beauty and warmth of my father's presence, and the blue flower I had so longed to touch. I felt my consciousness altering. My body grew light and then I was standing once again before the green pool in the beautiful garden. "Amisihathor," I called. "Are you there? Can you hear me?"

A breeze blew past my face. I heard a footfall, and turned around. A young woman in a blue cotton gown and golden sandals was coming towards me. She was wearing the lotus necklace and had a cylinder clutched in her hand, its leather cord twisted in her fingers. Her expressive face was so lovely and sad that it wounded me. I hugged her tightly. "Do not grieve, sister," I said. "You were always true to your heart. You loved deeply and never willingly hurt anyone. Why should you not be forgiven?"

Her body quivered. "I have not found peace," she whispered. "I cannot come before Osiris. I cannot find the way."

I stroked her silky hair. "That is because you have not let go. There was so much pain, I know. It was hard for you. I understand. But it is time now to let go of the pain. It is not your fault that Kamenwati made the wrong choices. The evil in his heart was not yours. You shared only love with him, and that was a beautiful thing. But it is a gift he is no longer worthy to receive. You performed maat by warning Kahotep. That man *is* worthy, and he loves you as you deserve to be loved. He is waiting to take you to the Field of Reeds. Raise your head, look, and you will see him."

I released her, and she glanced up with nervous hope. We saw him at the same time, and I heard her gasp of joy. I smiled as the priest approached. "Go," I said. "You will pass safely through the Underworld, and go into the Beautiful West. Live in peace for eternity."

She went to Kahotep, who embraced her. "Amisi," he said tenderly. "Do not spend eternity suffering for the mistakes of your husband. He fled with his life; where he wanders now, I do not know. But for you, I prepared a place with all honors. Everything was done to see you safely on your way. I called you wife in name, for so you are in my heart. Will you walk beside me? Will you come with me now?"

"I will." The voice was quiet and calm. "I am ready, my love. For the storm is over, is it not?"

He rested his forehead against hers. "Yes, Amisi," he answered softly. "The storm is over."

Hand in hand, they began to walk away, but not before they both looked back at me. The radiant happiness on their faces brought tears to my eyes. Kahotep made a sign of blessing, and

Amisihathor smiled. Then they were beyond my vision, and the whole scene faded away.

I took a deep breath, becoming aware of the room again, and felt the dampness on my cheeks. I had a deep sense of peace. Amisihathor was safe at last. I lay letting the calm wash over me, and realized that my most important decisions had been made. Glancing at the clock, I saw it was half-past three. Eight-thirty a.m. in England, and Ursula was an early riser. I placed the call that would complete the chain of events that she had started.

"Ursula," I said when she answered. "It's Lily. Are you busy? Good. Then sit down, and I'll tell you a story."

Glossary:

Amisi: (Ah-mee-see) – 'flower'. Amisihathor, the flower of Hathor, a songstress in the temple of Dendera.

Bastet: cat goddess linked with Hathor.

Hathor: goddess of love, beauty, women, and music. Worshipped in her temple at Dendera in Upper Egypt.

Horus: sky god, consort of Hathor, closely identified with kingship. Worshipped in his temple at Edfu, and at Dendera.

Kahotep: (Kah-ho-tep) – 'peaceful essence'. Chief scribe in the temple of Dendera.

Kamenwati: (Kah-men-wah-tee) — 'dark rebel'. Scribe in the temple of Edfu, later in Dendera. Husband to Amisihathor.

Kepi: (Kep-ee) — 'tempest'. A dancer in the temple of Dendera.

Meretsankh: (Merit-sawnk) — 'beloved life'. Child in the town of Dendera.

Re: the sun god, creator of life

Sister: a term of affection used by all Egyptians.

Made in the USA
Lexington, KY
20 July 2010